THE LONG FALL

THE LONG FALL

Lynn Kostoff

An Otto Penzler Book

Carroll & Graf Publishers
New York

THE LONG FALL

An Otto Penzler Book
Carroll & Graf Publishers
An Imprint of Avalon Publishing Group Inc.
161 William St., 16th Floor
New York, NY 10038

First Carroll & Graf edition 2003

All of the characters in this book are fictitious, and any resemblance to actual persons, living or dead, is purely coincidental.

Library of Congress Cataloging-in-Publication Data is available.

ISBN: 0-7867-1165-5

Book design by Paul Paddock
Printed in the United States of America
Distributed by Publishers Group West

This is for Lewis and Janet Kostoff.
With thanks to Melanie and Jeremy Kostoff, Marian Young
and Tom Pearson, and Otto Penzler.

Here is where we live.

Rickie Lee Jones, "The Albatross"

THE LONG FALL

ONE

Gut-shot, in the middle of his third death of the day, Jimmy Coates starts thinking about Nicole Braddock and the way her breasts torpedoed his chest when they were slow dancing at the Ocotillo Lounge the night before.

Jimmy had been camped out on a bar stool nursing a watery draft and trying to flesh out the scrawny hope that he could find a quick fix for what he owed Ray Harp before Ray went Darwinian in his collection practices. Then Nicole and six of her friends stepped through the door, a cadre of ASU students out slumming, over from Tempe for some midtown local color.

Jimmy hadn't paid much attention to them until a Tom-and-Jerry duo, sporting some thrift-store chic and working on their attitudes bummed a Marlboro and a light from him. They got to talking, and Jimmy let it be known that he'd paid his debt to society, and seeing the chance to raise their social deviance quotient a few points by hanging out with an ex-con, they invited Jimmy over to their table and began buying him drinks. No objection there, Jimmy switching from house drafts to tequila shooters and sunrises and giving them the standard gloss on life in the east wing of the Arizona State Prison Complex at Perryville.

Wanting to keep the drinks coming, Jimmy bulked up his story line, slapping on a little muscle and sinew to his original beef by borrowing another con's jacket, a mean little snake housed two cells down from him named Vince Treifoil, who was overly fond of entering banks and business establishments with firearms.

In actuality, Jimmy's last crime spree had unfolded and folded pretty much without a middle, no real second act to speak of. What sent him up was a black-market deal he'd worked out with a landscaping company to deliver an illegal tractor-trailer load of state-park-protected saguaro cacti to a new resort complex being built north of Sun City. After getting busted by the Staties for burnt-out brake lights, Jimmy unluckily caught a friend-of-the-earth judge who went on to hit him with twenty-four months, one for each of the saguaro in the bay of the tractor trailer.

At some point Tom or Jerry began feeding the juke, and eventually Jimmy found himself slow dancing with one Nicole Braddock, dark-haired and olive-skinned, the shapely daughter of a BMW dealer in Palm Springs and who was an absolute dead ringer for Jimmy's high school sweetheart, Jean Page—the same hair, eyes, mouth, skin—and in his arms Nicole felt like the stamp to his envelope, her head on his shoulder, Jimmy taking in the smell of her hair as they moved, Jimmy remembering all the make-out sessions with Jean, both of them seventeen, the universe running under their skin, and every necessary truth found in tongues and fingers and the sweet ache of breath, Jimmy dancing with a COD boner, and Nicole right there, not leaning away from it, Jimmy whispering in her ear, the music pouring around them, Jimmy not hearing the bass notes, only the melody line, and with Nicole pressed tight against him, Jimmy could conveniently ignore the arithmetic of passion, the very real fact obliterated by the false dawn of six rounds of tequila sunrises that the twenty-year-old girl in his arms could technically have been his daughter if Jean had run off and married him like he had asked her to instead of going along with her mom and old man's plans for her, Jimmy following the music instead, matching his moves to Nicole's, Jimmy leaning over and putting his lips on her neck, lightly kissing her hair, tasting perfume and the warmth of her skin, Jimmy whispering that it was a beautiful night for a ride in the desert, they could catch some stars, Cassiopeia on the rise and a new moon out there, just the two of them, Nicole shuddering under his touch and Jimmy closing his eyes, it taking him longer than it should have to realize the shudder came from her trying to stop laughing, because that's what she was doing, laughing, even while she kept her breasts pressed against him, she was laughing, Jimmy lifting his head and looking over at the table at her friends, all of them toasting Jimmy and Nicole and laughing, too, and that's when Nicole did it, put her hand gently on his cheek and in a low breathy voice told him that he was the genuine article, a true anachronism, one a girl like her found hard to resist, Nicole keeping her eyes locked on his, letting that little purr run loose behind her words, and Jimmy could see how much she was enjoying herself, how certain she was that someone like him wouldn't know what an anachronism was, the college girl toying with and putting one of the local yokels in his place, the whole thing a big joke, and Jimmy got pissed, leaned in and whispered, "This is your Local Color Station with a late-breaking bulletin. One day, honey-pie, you're going to wake up and discover those firm Tahitis you're now so proud of are sagging and chasing your navel, and you're going to panic and look around for that young Republican you married, but he's going to be on the seventeenth hole of the Scottsdale Country Club wielding his nine iron and working on his second coronary, and right then, when you're absolutely alone and up against it, you're going to remember this dance. It's going to ghost your bones." Jimmy kissed her cheek, then stepped back and walked out.

Now, though, Jimmy needs to get back to the business of dying. He's gut-shot and staggering in wide sloppy circles, waving his pistol, choking on each breath as he careens out of the saloon and into the wide dusty street, where he takes one in the shoulder and another in the chest and checks out under the hot eye of the noon sun.

When he gets up, he's dizzy, unable to focus for a moment on the wall of faces surrounding him until one swims into view, a red-haired kid with a small, sharp chin and green eyes. The kid leans down and starts waving a program in Jimmy's face.

Four hours later Jimmy's in the employee locker room rummaging through his pockets for some change. He hits the vending machine for a soda and catches a shot of himself in the mirror.

He looks like a fucking idiot. Black. Everything black. Cowboy hat, shirt, jeans, holster, boots. Black. Like someone's shadow or a charred tree trunk.

Six times a day he has to die. That's the way it is at Big and Bigger Jones's Old Wild West Park. Three showdowns and three shoot-outs per shift. The routines don't vary. As a bad guy, Jimmy makes the same dumb-ass moves in each show, the same ill-timed mistakes, growls out the same dying line when he's gunned down by the forces of frontier justice.

The all-black, though, that chafes Jimmy where he lives. He's sweating off three, four pounds a day and chewing up handfuls of salt tablets in the name of what? Realism? He can't believe any outlaw would be stupid enough to dress entirely in black and go out robbing stagecoaches and banks in temperatures over one hundred degrees.

The Native Americans are the ones with the sweet deal as far as Jimmy's concerned. The Jones brothers hired a passle of Pimas, Papagos, and Maricopas off the reservations, and all they had to do most of the day was walk around looking noble and tragic and man a few of the consession stands and restock the souvenir outposts. Best of all, they got to wear a loincloth and didn't have to worry about their nuts feeling like they'd been crammed in a toaster set on high an hour after they'd punched in.

Jimmy shakes his head and slots a quarter into the pay phone, and when Ray Harp picks up, Jimmy starts floating promises, saying he knows he's a little late, but a couple days, that's all he needs.

Ray doesn't say anything.

"Two days," Jimmy repeats.

Ray says,"It's not like you're going to get a monthly statement, Jimmy. I'm not MasterCard. It doesn't work that way. You know that."

A couple days, Jimmy promises, just until the payroll office at the Old Wild West cuts him his first paycheck. "It's yours, Ray, the whole thing. I'll drop it off same day."

More silence.

"Look," Jimmy says. "The first check's yours, okay? I'm working my ass off here, dying six times a day for it."

"I can fix it, Jimmy, so you only have to do it once." A second later, Ray hangs up.

Jimmy heads back to his locker and starts undressing. He's still sweating. He digs out more change, and with his shirt flapping around him, goes over to the vending machine and guzzles another soda. The carbonation leaves his throat feeling scoured and the inside of his nose burning.

He's catching little whiffs of himself, and the picture isn't pretty. His pores are leaking the residue of last night's tequila follies and the equivalent of fast-food carbon dating for the half life of Big Macs and the Colonel's Extra Crispy. Everything's kicked up a metabolic notch from a small hit of speed he took after noon to help him get through his last three deaths.

Russ Crawford, the general manager, walks over to Jimmy's locker and says, "They want to see you upstairs."

Jimmy shakes his head. "I've already punched out. And I need a shower. I'll stop on my way out."

"Upstairs," Crawford says. "As in five minutes ago."

Crawford's in his early forties and reminds Jimmy of a squirrel. The guy's head is way too small for the rest of him. Wearing chaps and a cowboy hat doesn't help matters much either.

"Hey, Russ," Jimmy says. "Let me ask you something. You know what an anachronism is?"

Russ waves the question away. "I don't want to talk about spiders. I got a job to do."

Jimmy's been doing an informal survey all day. So far he's been told an anachronism is the brand name for a new line of racing tires, a flower, a street in Glendale, a rock band, and an over-the-counter antibiotic cream for yeast infections.

Jimmy knocks his locker shut and heads for the stairs, pausing along the way to grab another soda, which he polishes off while he hurriedly rebuttons his shirt one-handed. The back of his neck is tightening up, and one of his black cowboy boots has begun to squeak.

The receptionist in the main office is wearing a short buckskin dress and pale pink lipstick. Her hair's a light brown and French-braided. She has a long, elegantly tapered neck that would give Dracula the squirts just looking at it. Jimmy's trying to figure out if she's wearing a bra when she tells him the Jones brothers are expecting him.

Her body language is difficult to get a read on until Jimmy finally figures out she's trying to stay upwind of him.

"Hard day on the range," he says, topping it off with a light shrug. The follow-up smile, a killer he's practiced and perfected, is lost on her when she swivels in her chair and goes back to her computer. On the screen is a video poker game. A full house is showing.

Jimmy Coates knocks and then steps into Big and Bigger Jones's office. It's got a high stippled ceiling with exposed beams, hardwood floors with Navajo rugs, and a large picture window overlooking the main street of the Old Wild West Park. Dominating the center of the office is a long polished desk that looks like it's been cut from a sequoia.

The Jones brothers stand up and wave him into a chair.

The brothers are twins who were born five minutes apart. The first was Big. The second was Bigger. From what Jimmy can see, they've managed to live up to their names. They look like massive balls of suet squeezed into identical soft gray Western-cut suits. They're wearing matching gray Stetsons and monogrammed bolo ties. It looks like he's interrupted snack time. Each of them's holding a partially pillaged bag of Doritos.

"We appreciate you dropping by, Mr. Catz," Big says.

"Coates," Jimmy says. "The name's Coates."

Bigger slides over an open folder, and Big glances down and somehow manages to nod and shrug at the same time.

"It doesn't appear you've been with us long," Bigger says, tapping the file.

"One week and change," Jimmy says. "You boys have something nice going here. We've been packing them in every day."

"Families," Big says. "It's families who visit the Old Wild West."

"Lots of families," Bigger adds. "Families looking for family-type entertainment."

"Families," Jimmy says. "I'm with you so far, boys."

Big squints at the file, then lifts his head. Jimmy finds it hard to make eye contact with either brother. Their eyes are small, the color of wet coffee grounds, and spaced wide and high in their faces. Even when you're fronting them, it's like they're trying to look around you at something behind your back.

"While families are enjoying this family entertainment," Big says, "they do not appreciate erratic or irresponsible behavior on the part of those providing the family entertainment."

"Look," Jimmy says, "if you're referring to that brood from Terre Haute, I talked to the dad afterward. We got it all straightened out."

"We're referring to twelve-year-old children and mammary glands," Bigger says. "Specifically, the grandson of the governor, who visited the Old West as part of his birthday celebration and who was in attendance at the twelve o'clock shoot-out."

"And who asked you to sign his program," Big adds.

"Which I did," Jimmy says, puzzled.

"With this." Bigger slips his hand inside his suit jacket and holds a pen aloft. On its side is a photo of Pete Samoa's second wife, Doris, in a black one-piece. Bigger upends the pen, and the black one-piece disappears, giving Jimmy and the Jones brothers a glimpse at the wonders of silicone and Doris's fabled chest.

Jimmy raises his hand. "An honest mistake."

"Policy at the Old Wild West explicitly states that employees are to leave all personal items in the locker room during the performance of their duties." Big pauses and looks at his brother, who's still holding the pen aloft. "And concerning writing implements, personnel are to use and distribute, when appropriate, gratis to the public, only those writing implements bearing the logo and trademark of the Old Wild West." Big pulls out one of the park's pens and holds it up.

"There are no exceptions to policy, Mr. Coast," Bigger says.

"The same size and shape there," Jimmy says, pointing at the pens. "Easy enough to get them confused, you're in a hurry."

"Fortunately our general manager, Russ Crawford, was able to divert the boy with the promise of an additional tomahawk and thus regain possession of the pen without drawing the attention of the media covering the birthday visit," Big says.

A raw deal for the kid, Jimmy thinks. *A plastic tomahawk for a perpetual titty show.*

"Is that a smile, Mr. Cortez?" Bigger asks. "Is there something humorous or amusing that neither my brother nor I are aware of in the potential negative attendant publicity resulting from one of our gunslingers passing out pens festooned with bared mammary glands and advertising dubious enterprises like pawn shops to the grandson of the man holding the highest office in the state?"

"A man who before taking that office was an ordained Baptist minister," Big adds.

"Relief," Jimmy says, backpedalling. "My expression there, it's relief because I'm relieved everything turned out all right."

"As regards to the erratic and irresponsible behavior," Big starts in.

"Thing of the past," Jimmy says quickly. "Rest assured, boys."

Big fingers his bolo tie and looks at his brother. Jimmy keeps his eyes aimed at the wall behind them. It's covered in framed photographs, a scattering of hostage celebrity shots, the brothers shaking hands with a bunch of has-beens, a roster of over-the-hill ballplayers, a choir of third-rate Vegas crooners, some television and movie zeroes, and a hearty salting of state and city politicos.

"Is there a problem with our cooling system we're not aware of, Mr. Costs?" Bigger asks.

"Uh, I don't think so." Jimmy glances around the office. "Why do you ask?" He feels like he's back in the fourth grade, Mrs. Dell about to swoop down and trip him up with some trick question, one usually dealing with the metric system. Mrs. Dell, she was a big fan of measurement.

"You're sweating," Big says.

"A lot," Bigger adds.

"I got a quirky metabolism." When Jimmy glances down, he notices he'd buttoned his shirt wrong on the way to the office earlier. It looks like a mangled kite.

That's when he notices something else: His bladder's begun to send out distress calls, some SOS action on account of all those sodas earlier.

Big reaches down and rustles a couple of papers in the file. "My brother and I have always prided ourselves on being community-oriented. Phoenix has been good to us. We like to believe we've been good for Phoenix. That's the working principle behind our hiring practices. We believe in giving people a chance." Big pauses, then adds, "We've had a number of ex-convicts on our payroll over the years."

"They were grateful for the chance and our faith in them," Bigger joins in. "No erratic behavior on their parts is how I'd put it."

"You boys are known for giving someone a fair shake," Jimmy says. "Absolutely. Your reputation precedes you."

"Unfortunately so has yours," Big says, "and you appear to have caught up with it."

"I've paid my debt to society." Jimmy shifts into contrition and presses the gas on the sincerity.

"We'd like to believe you," Big says.

"You can take it to the bank." Jimmy rises from the chair and nods twice.

"Good," Bigger says. "Then we're sure you won't mind accompanying Ms. Wing to the nurse's station."

"Huh?" Jimmy says. "Not necessary. This sweating, like I was telling you boys, I got a quirky metabolism." He steps up to the desk and extends his hand. "Nothing a good cold shower won't cure."

"We were thinking more along the lines of a urine sample," Big says. "A little lab work."

Oh, shit, Jimmy thinks.

"Fine there. No problem," Jimmy says, stepping back. "But what say, boys, we put that on the docket first thing tomorrow morning? See, I've already punched out, and I need to get cleaned up and going here. I'm running a little late for an appointment."

"I think this afternoon would be better," Big says.

"Won't take more than a few minutes of your time." Big closes Jimmy's file.

Jimmy's cataloging the probable results of a drug test. It'll be the equivalent of a chemical spill that would make the EPA blush.

"I'd like to oblige you boys," he begins slowly.

"Then do," Big says.

They're standing side by side, watching him.

If they weren't so obviously enjoying this little session, Jimmy thinks, maybe he could hunker down and turn things around. He's talked his way out of tighter places before. And he's capable of doing it again. He knows that. But the thing is, they're enjoying it so much, clamping him, and over a dipshit job barely a click over minimum wage.

Big clears his throat.

They're waiting for him to beg. Jimmy can read it in both their faces. Beg them for the chance to keep dressing up in a black cowboy outfit and shoot it out six times a day for the amusement of the citizens. They're waiting, looking forward to it. They want him to beg.

"Tell you what, boys," Jimmy says, "why don't you let me save us all a little time?"

Jimmy steps back in front of the desk. He plays the smile large.

The brothers glance at each other. Big clears his throat again.

Jimmy leans closer, then snags an Old West coffee mug and slides it to the edge of the desk. "Yes, sir," he says, "let's just cut right to the chase." In two quick moves, he has the zipper of the black jeans down and his dick out.

"Whoa there," Bigger says.

Big makes a stab at snatching back the mug, but Jimmy's too fast for him. Or rather, all the sodas he's guzzled this afternoon are. The faucet's full on now, and Jimmy's feeling good.

He's also a little reckless with his aim.

Big and Bigger each make a grab for the phone, but finally retreat to the wall of photographs. Big is holding Jimmy's personnel file to his chest like a shield.

Jimmy leans into the job, putting a sizzling head on the mug and then switching over to a nearby pencil holder.

Jimmy's feeling good, yes he is, until he suddenly hears Ray Harp's voice echoing in his head: *It's not like you're going to get a monthly statement, Jimmy. I'm not MasterCard. It doesn't work that way.*

And Jimmy, trying to avoid snagging his dick on the zipper as he tucks himself back in, knows that this time he's really up against it.

This time he's pissed more than a paycheck away.

TWO

Evelyn Coates struggles to locate and then resurrect her flight-attendant's smile each time the bell above the door rings and a customer enters. The smile is important. It's important never to forget that. People want to feel important, and therefore it's important to give people what they want. Giving people what they want creates satisfied customers, and satisfied customers are repeat customers, and repeat customers are important, the lifeblood of any business.

She's trying. She really is. The smile, though, just gets harder to find and hold.

Evelyn glances up at the clock and adjusts the neckline of the pale green smock she wears over her skirt and blouse. On the counter, bracketing her, are two cardboard placards, one advertising senior citizen discounts, the other detailing the store's policy on unclaimed apparel.

Over the last month, Evelyn's been rotating among the branches of Frontier Cleaners, getting a feel for the clientele and employees at each store, learning the basic duties behind running and operating the chain, soaking up the business from the inside out, as her husband likes to say, a portion of her evenings devoted to reviewing the long- and short-term plans Richard envisions, one of which is Evelyn eventually becoming a full partner in the business.

It's not like she stepped into the dry-cleaning business expecting it to be glamorous or exciting. It simply made a kind of sense, after she quit the airlines, not so much a step as a half step, the type of decision, she now realizes, that has come to inform the life Richard and she have made together.

A comfortable life. A good life. A sensible life. One spent balancing the practical and the passionate.

Evelyn glances at the clock again. Three customers come in. Evelyn waits on them, tagging clothes, handing out claim checks, verifying names, addresses, phone numbers, and making note of any special instructions. She's conscious of the manager, Maria Sandover, hovering near the revolving racks of the day's pickups, watching her.

There's another lull in customer traffic. Evelyn looks up at the clock. 1:27. The hands have moved, but the time hasn't seemed to change. She's supposed to stay until five today and then meet Richard for dinner.

Maria Sandover steps up next to the register. Evelyn figures she's somewhere in her early forties, but everything in her bearing makes her seem older: the dark hair shadowed by premature gray, no makeup to speak of, a pair of heavy unflattering glasses, a dark blue checked dress falling to midcalf, sensible shoes.

"You forgot to mention the ten percent discount on Mondays," Maria says. "With each transaction, you should remind the customer of the standard and special discounts for the week. It's also important to wish each customer a good day. You neglected to do that twice today."

For some reason, Evelyn thinks of the fan of fold-out photographs, school shots of five boys, that Maria had brought out to show Evelyn on more than one occasion as if she were demonstrating features on a car. The Sandover brood ranged from five to eighteen. Evelyn thought she made the appropriate murmurs of approval, but now she's not so sure. She's been doing that a lot lately, becoming impatient or distracted and making small missteps in manners and social niceties that she only becomes aware of much later, after the fact.

Earlier last week when she'd once again been late getting to the store, Evelyn had overheard Maria Sandover talking with some of the other employees in the break room. They'd been discussing Richard and her.

The consensus on Richard held no surprises. As a boss, he was demanding and exacting, but he was also scrupulously fair and even-handed in employee relations and had earned their respect and loyalty. He appreciated a job done well and was not afraid to roll up his sleeves and help out when things got tight. He made it a point to be on a first-name basis with everyone who worked for him and knew where they lived, the names of spouses and children or their boyfriends and girlfriends. He remembered birthdays and anniversaries. He paid above minimum wage and set up a generous benefits package. He was a good man, a hardworking man, who expected the best from himself and others around him.

What Evelyn had overheard about herself was a different story. She's vain. Full of herself. Alternately aloof or condescending. Tempermental. She doesn't pull her weight around the store. She flirts with customers. She ignores customers. She wears too much makeup. Her dresses are too tight. She laughs too much or too little. She's pampered. Afraid to get her hands dirty. She's headstrong. A pretty package with nothing inside.

At first, Evelyn had been shocked and hurt and dismayed by what she'd heard. There had to have been some mistake. She'd tried to be pleasant. She'd tried to get along. Somehow she'd failed horribly at both.

Eventually, though, something odd happened. She came to like those gossipy reactions, even take an odd sort of pride in them.

Suddenly she was a Bad Girl.

She again glances up at the clock. 1:45. Evelyn walks back to the break room. It's empty. There's a pot of coffee brewing, and the portable television in the corner is still on, tuned to an afternoon talk show. It's a segment on Big Wish kids, five of them, three boys and two girls, all twelve and under, with terminal illnesses.

One of the boys says, "Sometimes when I wake up in the morning, it feels like there's a fire in my bones." He's named Timmy and he's eight years old, and he goes on to say he wants to visit the Grand Canyon and the Petrified Forest.

There's a long sibilant hiss as the coffee finishes brewing. Evelyn closes her eyes for a moment and then crosses the room and turns off the television.

She walks back down the hall to the employee restroom. She locks herself in the first stall, lets out her breath, then sits down. She stretches her arms, pressing her hands on the walls to either side of her, then drops them back into her lap.

She watches the second hand circle the face of her watch.

She tries to imagine the need for a Big Wish and what hers would be.

THREE

The sun's burning away what's left of the morning, and the needle on the gas gauge is kissing empty when Jimmy pulls into the lot at Pete Samoa's Pawn Emporium. There's one other car parked out front.

Most of the surrounding buildings are one story and flat-roofed, fading and dirty and rundown, like paint was a relative they'd lost track of. A donut joint, a used tire shop, a twenty-four-hour Laundromat, a check-cashing service, and a package store are sandwiched between a string of empty storefronts covered in gang graffiti, obscenities, and oddly sequenced numbers resembling zip codes.

Just beyond a lethargic traffic light is a sun-baked playground empty of children but crawling with stray cats. At a glance, Jimmy figures there must be thirty or forty of them milling about, all of them scrawny and mange-ridden and yowling. At the edge of the grounds is an old man in a baseball cap, who's methodically throwing pieces of gravel and chips of concrete at the cats and singing.

Jimmy burns down a Marlboro waiting for the owner of the other car to come out of the emporium and leave. He then flips back a canvas tarp in the truck bed and carries in a twenty-one-inch color television, a VCR, three CD players, a PC, and two plastic garbage bags filled with hubcaps.

Pete Samoa's perched on a metal stool behind the long glass-faced counter fronting the register, his posture reminding Jimmy of a buzzard with its wings folded.

Nothing about Pete Samoa ever seemed to change. A little more gray at the temples now, but the same steel-rimmed bifocals punched back on his nose; the dark, sun-cured skin; the asymmetrical pencil-thin goatee resembling dried lines of chocolate syrup. The wardrobe's a ditto, too. Blue pocket-T, plaid baggy Bermudas, black mesh shoes. A tiny gold crucifix lying in the hollow of his throat.

Pete climbs down from the stool and walks around the counter. He pulls a stub of a number two pencil from behind his ear and a small notebook from his pocket and begins itemizing what Jimmy's set on the floor.

Jimmy looks around the emporium. Nothing's changed there either. Row upon row of narrow and cluttered metal shelves filled with dusty hard-luck bargains. Half the fluorescent lights lining the ceiling burnt-out or buzzing. The stuff here, the straight pawn, covers the rent and utilities on the shop. What Jimmy brought in will end up in one of Pete's three warehouses over in Avondale and will be fenced out within forty-eight hours.

Pete walks back around the counter, writes down a figure, rips the page from his notebook, and slides it across to Jimmy.

Jimmy glances at it, then looks down at his shoes. He then pulls a white handkerchief from his back pocket and offers it to Pete.

"I was thinking maybe you needed that for your glasses," he says. "You know, maybe you had a speck on the lens there that you confused with a decimal point."

Pete crosses his arms on his chest. "Glasses are fine, Jimmy."

"Maybe it's the light then," Jimmy says, sliding the paper back across the counter. "You being too fucking cheap to replace the bulbs, the place like a cave here, you got some numbers reversed."

"Best I can do," Pete says, nodding at the slip of paper.

Next to the cash register is a plastic cup full of pens, the name of the shop and phone number on one side, the other holding a photo of an overly made-up middle-aged woman with an upswept mass of hair the color of butter. She's wearing a black one-piece bathing suit that's about two sizes too small. Jimmy lifts a pen and tilts it and watches the bathing suit drain away.

Pete shakes the cup and winks. "That's Doris. The new Missus."

Pete had been passing pens out at the Ocotillo the other night, and Jimmy supposes if you look at it from one perspective, shave away a few extenuating circumstances, you could see Pete Samoa as the prime mover in the series of events leading to Jimmy losing his job at the Old Wild West and Pete therefore owing him one.

"A little deeper in the pockets," Jimmy says, dropping the pen back into the cup. "Come on."

"What, come on? I'm looking at amateur hour here. What you do, hit one of the student ghettos over at Tempe?" Pete punches back his bifocals. "This is an embarrassment, Jimmy. At least bring me something I can work with."

"A big score, huh, Pete, like maybe a tractor-trailer load of government-protected saguaros? A sure thing, that one. I follow up on your tip and end up looking at twenty-four months in Perryville."

Pete shrugs. "No one twisted your arm. I heard something. I passed it on. It was entirely up to you what you did with that knowledge."

Jimmy bites his lower lip and looks around the store, then turns back to the counter and picks up the slip of paper, studies it, puts it back down, and then picks it up again.

"Okay. Fine. Right there. Okay," Jimmy says.

The thing is, on one level, Jimmy knows Pete's right. A couple trash bags of hubcaps and some low-tech toys are strictly bottom-end action, a definite embarrassment, but until he can get a few things realigned, Jimmy needs some walking-around money.

Pete doesn't punch up the sale on the register. Instead he brings out a squat metal box with a combo lock. He turns his back to open it. Jimmy watches him count out the bills.

"What the hell you doing?" he asks when Pete finishes. "You think I'm rusty on my basic math skills? That maybe I forgot how to add?"

Pete holds up an index finger. He pulls a small handgun from the front right pocket of his Bermudas and lays it next to the cash. "I thought you might want to take the balance out in trade," he says.

"Why would you think that?" It's a shitty little .22, the bluing on the barrel gone, the grip cracked and mended with electrical tape.

Pete looks up at the ceiling. "Because, Jimmy, I hear things. I stand behind this counter, and sometimes I sell things and sometimes I buy things, but mostly what I do is hear things. Your name and Ray Harp's, for example," he says, "have come up more than once of late, friend."

Jimmy looks out toward the parking lot.

"Ray's been on edge for a while now, " Pete says. "Things are tense between him and some of the Mexican gangs running crank labs. They aren't very happy with the way Ray's cutting up the pie."

"What's that got to do with me?"

"I shouldn't have to explain this to you, Jimmy," Pete says, dropping his hand and tapping the cylinder on the .22. "What I'm saying here is Ray has become more focused in his business practices since you went up. Considerably more focused. He can't afford not to be. The Mex gangs are watching him, looking for any signs of weakness."

You pick up a gun, Jimmy thinks, *and it has a way of getting used.* He nudges the .22 over to Pete's side of the counter. "I appreciate the thought, but I think I'll stick with the cash."

"Even if Ray has Newt Deems and Aaron Limbe out looking for you?" Pete asks, counting out the rest of the bills.

Jimmy starts rubbing the top of his head. Newt's straight muscle. Jimmy can understand him coming around. But Aaron Limbe is a different story. He's a wrinkle no iron can touch.

"Limbe's working for Ray now?" Jimmy asks.

Pete nods.

"Look, do me a favor, will you?" Jimmy pulls the cash across the counter and crams it in the front pocket of his jeans. "If Newt or Limbe, they come back in here asking about me, you tell them as far as you know, everything's copacetic, okay? Can you do that?"

Pete slowly lets out his breath and nods. "That's as far as it goes though," he says.

"I appreciate that. I really do." Jimmy starts rubbing the top of his head again. "I may have gotten off on the wrong foot with Ray, but I'm working on straightening things out."

Pete's smiling but won't look him in the eye. "I'm glad to hear that, Jimmy."

Jimmy digs out his truck keys and turns to leave.

He's just about made the door when Pete calls out to him. "Hey, I almost forgot. Sorry to hear about your old man. A hell of a thing, that. They let you out for the funeral?"

"No." Jimmy leaves it at that. The last thing he wants is to get into a discussion about his father.

He palms the doorknob and tells Pete he'll see him around.

Outside, the sun's so bright it's like a slap.

FOUR

Jimmy's brother, Richard, owns and runs a string of dry-cleaning stores and keeps a central office in downtown Phoenix in a dark, somber, turn-of-the-century, stone building. From where Jimmy's sitting he can look out the window past lines of palms and eucalypti and see snatches of traffic on Washington and beyond that, part of Wesley Brolin Plaza and the bright copper dome of the old capitol building with the white angel of mercy statue perched on its top like half of a wedding cake decoration.

Jimmy fights back a yawn. It's 7:45, and he didn't have time to grab coffee, let alone breakfast, to make the meeting with his brother on time. Harriett, the receptionist, had some decaf brewing, but Jimmy had passed on that one. As far as he's concerned, decaf's the equivalent of Elvis impersonators and Christian rock bands. All of them in one way or another missed the point.

A couple minutes later Jimmy hears the door open behind him, and Richard walks briskly across the office and stands behind his desk. Richard and Jimmy have never looked anything alike, not even as kids. Their father used to say that their genetic magnetic poles were reversed. Richard gets his looks from their mother and her side of the family. He's tall and lanky, pushing six-four, one of those long-distance-runner physiques, with fair skin and fine straight hair not quite brown or blond, bones set close under the skin and sharpening his features. Jimmy, well, he's always been close to the ground, five-eight in his socks, dark and thick, black hair and two shaves a day like the old man. Swarthy, his mom called him.

Richard's wearing one of those tan lightweight khaki suits with ruler-straight creases, a pale blue shirt, and a dark knit tie. He takes in Jimmy's sneakers, jeans, and T-shirt with a glance and sits down.

"I wondered how long it would take," he says.

"Nice to see you, too," Jimmy says.

Richard lets that one go by. He turns and boots up his computer. The logo for Frontier Cleaners flashes on the screen—a neon saguaro cactus with a citrus-colored sun perched on its top right arm—followed by a quick burst of music that Jimmy doesn't recognize.

Richard swivels his head and studies him, then goes back to the computer screen, clicking on his e-mail and typing in a password. "I'm assuming this visit's about dad's estate and why you're just getting around to doing something about it."

"Hey, I'm here. Okay?"

"Not okay, Jimmy. Far from okay." Richard slides his chair back behind the desk. "Did you know the back taxes and your share of the probate costs are due on the West Dobbins parcel before the end of the month? Any ideas on how you plan to pay them?"

"I'm working on it." Jimmy glances at his watch. Fifteen minutes. About the average before he feels like punching out his brother. Even as a kid, Richard had the superior attitude. Mr. Chapter and Verse. Mr. Median Strip to Jimmy's passing lanes.

"I knew it would come to this," Richard says.

Jimmy tries to ignore the growling in his stomach while Richard checks in with his lecture mode, pointing out what Jimmy's already aware of, that unless he can find the cash to cover the back taxes, he'll lose his share of the inheritance. The farmhouse and the twenty acres it sits on will end up auctioned off. Richard tells him the developers have already picked up the scent and begun circling like wolves.

"That land's been in the family for three generations," Richard adds. "I don't know what dad was thinking when he left it to you."

"Grandpa," Jimmy says. "He did it because Grandpa wanted me to have it."

"And now you're going to uphold the tradition of fucking up just like he did." Richard again can't keep himself from pushing things in Jimmy's face, citing the obvious family parallels between Jimmy and his namesake, James Earl Coates, who at one time had been one of the largest cattle ranchers in the Maricopa Valley and who in a gaudy and inglorious trajectory of high living and poor planning had gone on to lose the bulk of the land and assets he'd amassed during his seventy-nine years.

"So what are you going to do?" Richard asks.

"You're really enjoying this, aren't you?"

Richard leans back in his chair. "Enjoyable is not exactly how I'd characterize a visit with you, Jimmy. Predictable, maybe. Tiresome, certainly." Richard stretches, latching his fingers behind his neck.

The thing is, if Penny Hardaway had not scored twenty-nine points against the Lakers, Jimmy would not be having this conversation. He'd be a man of property, dotted-line time, free and clear. He would have had the back taxes and probate costs covered, and he would not have to be enduring his brother's sanctimonious bullshit.

When he got out of Perryville, Jimmy had borrowed six grand from Ray Harp, Jimmy going in at six-and-a-half for five, willing to live with the twenty-five percent interest and Ray's clock because Jimmy knew once he got the taxes paid off and the land formally in his name he could walk into a bank of choice and, given its development potential, get a loan against the property with no problem and then simply go on and pay back Ray. It was a workable plan, a necessary, if roundabout, way for an ex-con with an apocalyptic credit history to secure a loan along conventional lines.

After he got the money from Ray, Jimmy had every intention

of going straight to the tax office, but then he ran into a speed bump of a waitress named Marci, who introduced him to a friend of her brother's, a guy named Carl Bailey, who she said worked as a trainer for the Phoenix Suns, it eventually turning out Carl was not exactly a trainer but more like an assistant to an assistant of the Suns' trainer, but the way Jimmy saw it, the guy was still hanging out at America West with the team and should have known the skinny on the players no matter what his official title was.

Over drinks, Carl confided that Penny Hardaway had recently pulled the hamstring in his right thigh during practice, but that the general manager and the coaching staff had elected to keep quiet about the injury. Hardaway had been burning up the nets, and with the Western Conference playoffs starting, they weren't about to give L.A. any psychological edge by admitting that Hardaway was hurt. He was still slated to start against the Lakers. Carl said Penny would be lucky to finish the first quarter before being benched.

Carl didn't need to explain to Jimmy how this type of inside info could benefit an individual so inclined to bet against the point spread set for the next game, as well as laying down a sizable side bet on Hardaway's projected total for the night itself. Jimmy figured that one out all by himself.

Jimmy had watched the game with the regulars at the Chute, a bunch of die-hard Suns fans, and had basked in their groans and curses as Phoenix consistently choked on both offense and defense during the first half. Hardaway went to the bench in the middle of the second quarter, having gone one for twelve from the field. By halftime the Lakers were up sixteen points.

Everything fell apart for Jimmy in the second half when the Suns decided to play basketball. The TV commentators kept using words like "decisive," "inspired," and "heroic." The regulars at the Chute yelled themselves hoarse while Jimmy sat clutching his draft in disbelief, Hardaway setting off a twenty-two-point run in the third quarter, Hardaway playing in some zone beyond his injury, the Suns going on to win by two. For Jimmy, the win had been less important than the fact that the original point spread had been reestablished.

Jimmy's financial problems kept compounding. After having lost what he'd borrowed from Ray Harp on the game, he missed the first scheduled repayment deadline. The tax problem on his inheritance still loomed. Until he could scare up another idea for some quick cash, Jimmy had been desperate enough to take a regular job, but even that had backfired when the Jones brothers cut him loose from the Old Wild West Park, and Jimmy found himself running out of what he'd had in oceanic abundance at Perryville Correctional: time.

Which is why he's ended up in his brother's office, Jimmy grinding his teeth and having to listen to Richard as he paces around the room like a prosecuting attorney building a case.

"It never stops, and you never learn," Richard says, pausing by the corner of the desk. Just behind and to his left, the screen saver on the computer pops up.

Jimmy gets up and walks past Richard, then bends over and squints at the screen. It holds six photos shrunken to the size of playing cards. Standard family stuff of their mother and father and Richard's wife, Evelyn, and one of Richard at the groundbreaking for the first Frontier Cleaners.

Jimmy's momentarily distracted by a shot of Evelyn in a scooped-neck blue dress—she's a former airline attendant and had a pair on her that would make a blind man weep—before he notices the screen does not contain a single shot of him. He's AWOL from every photo, cropped from Richard's miniature pictorial family history.

Jimmy's stomach starts growling again.

Richard's still waiting for him to say something.

Jimmy walks back to his seat.

"You can't do it, can you?" Richard asks. "You show up here, but you can't bring yourself to ask. What do you expect me to do? Blind myself like dad and then go on and clean up after you and pretend it's going to make a difference this time?"

"Let's leave dad out of this," Jimmy says. "You've made your point."

"You really think it's that simple, don't you?"

The money part was, Jimmy thinks. Money is always simple. You either have it or you don't. If you have it, you spend it. If you don't, you find a way to get some. It was Richard's long dot-every-i memory that complicated things. That and the fact that when it came to passing judgment on anything, Richard had two favorite colors: black and white.

Jimmy watches Richard move behind the desk again. He steeples his fingers, then looks out the window and back at Jimmy.

"I'm not doing this for you, you know."

Richard adjusts his cuffs and then slides a sheath of papers across the desk. "You want to sign those, Jimmy, I can start the follow-up."

Jimmy leans forward in his chair. "Papers?" he asks. "I thought you were going to cut a check, like a loan."

"Dad named me executor of the estate, Jimmy. I'm working with his lawyer, Ben Caplan, through all the probate hassles. Things are badly tangled."

Jimmy nods, but he can't untrack the thought that he'd be walking out of the office with a check.

"What are the papers for?" he asks finally.

"Power of attorney. You sign them, and I'll be authorized to settle your end of the inheritance. I'll pass the check on to Caplan, and he can push through the paperwork on the back taxes and probate costs and keep the Dobbins parcel off the auction block."

"I guess so," Jimmy says. "How long's this going to take?"

"I told you, Caplan's a good attorney. A personal friend, too. He'll get it done quickly and efficiently."

Jimmy balks some more, his misgivings mixing with thoughts of Ray Harp and the deadlines Jimmy's missed, Ray working on a different clock from Richard and this Caplan guy.

"What's the problem now, Jimmy?" The patience is leaking

out of Richard's voice, and he's begun lightly tapping the edge of the desk, the fingers of his right hand soft but insistent.

"I don't know. I just didn't think it would be this complicated," Jimmy says.

"What do you want me to do? Remember, you came to me, Jimmy. You have some other way to cover what's owed on the Dobbins parcel, that's fine." Richard pauses, letting the silence take on some weight before going on. "Given your track record on repaying personal loans, I'd prefer that."

"Okay, okay," Jimmy says, wanting to avoid that particular stretch of road. He gestures toward the papers. "I get copies, right?"

"Of course." Richard takes out a pen from the inside pocket of his jacket and buzzes Harriet, his secretary, to come in and witness.

Jimmy's figuring he can take his copy of the agreement and show Ray Harp, use it as a combo stalling tactic and good-faith gesture, some black-and-white proof that Jimmy's good for what he owes. Whatever else he may be, Ray Harp is also a businessman, and he's bound to appreciate what the Dobbins property is worth.

Richard looks over at the clock and then holds up the pen.

Jimmy takes the pen and leans over the desk. He signs where Richard tells him, Harriett hovering over his shoulder, reminding him of a battery of elementary school teachers who were always on his case about one thing or another. Jimmy keeps expecting her to ambush him on penmanship.

Richard separates the paperwork into two piles, and then Harriet slides Jimmy's copy into a manila envelope and sets it on the corner of the desk and leaves without a word.

Jimmy looks down at the pen in his hand and then at Richard, who's moved from the desk to the window, where he's standing with his back to him.

Richard asks him if he's been out to the cemetery yet. "What did you think of the stone? The angels on either end too much?"

"Nah," Jimmy says. "They're fine."

Richard glances back over his shoulder and smiles. "There are no angels on the stone, Jimmy. It's a simple granite marker. Name and dates, that's all."

"Bingo," Jimmy says. "You win, Richard."

"There are times," Richard says, turning back to the window, "when I almost feel sorry for you, Jimmy. Fortunately, they don't last long."

Jimmy looks over at the screen saver with the family photos on the computer, him missing-in-action in all of them, then down at the manila envelope in his hand.

"What did you do, Richard?"

Richard waits awhile before answering. "What I knew I had to. What everybody in the family has always had to do. Save you from yourself."

Jimmy tears into the manila envelope and starts rummaging through the paperwork, but the print keeps sliding all over the page and the pages themselves dividing and subdividing, multiplying like amoebas.

"What did I sign, Richard?" Jimmy's voice a combo platter of desperation, anger, and panic.

"Listen to yourself." Richard remains at the window. "The fact that you have to ask a question like that just proves my point."

"That's what this all comes down to. Not me. You. You being right. You proving a point."

"What I did, I did for your own good, Jimmy."

"Fuck my own good. The old man left the Dobbins parcel to me. It's mine."

"There's the spirit of the law and then the letter of the law. And I believe in this case the probate judge knows his alphabet, Jimmy."

"I don't care. It's mine, Richard. You know that."

"Okay," Richard says, turning and facing Jimmy. "For the sake of argument, let's agree the land's yours and I'm just holding it temporarily in escrow. How's that sound? Fair enough?"

"What's the catch?" Jimmy says, knowing there has to be one with Richard.

"The property reverts to you in five years," Richard says. "I'll even pay the taxes during the interim. All you have to do is stay out of trouble. You get a job, you keep it, and you function like a responsible adult. In five years the property's yours, free and clear. What do you think?"

Jimmy doesn't say anything.

Richard shakes his head and turns back to the window. "Five years too daunting a prospect for you, Jimmy? How about three then? Think you could handle that? One thousand ninety-five days of reasonable behavior? Or do we need to shave a few more off? You have any suggestions, a ballpark figure, say, for how long you could sustain acting your age and out of trouble?"

"You prick," Jimmy says quietly.

Richard lets out a short, dry laugh. "You think I couldn't figure out why you were in such a hurry to get those taxes cleared and the land officially in your name, Jimmy? How bad is it this time, the trouble you've gotten yourself into?"

How bad, Jimmy thinks, and wonders how Richard and his rational universe would deal with the imminent arrival of Aaron Limbe and Newt Deems, the agent and arm of Ray Harp's worst impulses and general business practices.

"Bad," Jimmy says finally and leaves it at that, not wanting to give Richard the satisfaction of further details.

"I can't carry you on this one," his brother says.

"Can't or won't?"

"Take your pick," Richard says.

"You're something," Jimmy says. "The whole time, you standing there with your back to me. You have all the answers, but you can't talk and look me in the eye at the same time."

Another short, dry laugh. "That's it, huh? That's what you think?"

Before Jimmy can fully register the movement, Richard has moved from the window and crossed the room, Jimmy not ready for what he sees next, Richard's face contorted, its features distended in rage, Richard giving in to, bowing before it, a rage that's been cooked deep in the marrow.

Without thinking, Jimmy takes a step back.

"You weren't there," Richard says. "Not then. Not ever. Not when it counted."

Richard lifts his arm and points at Jimmy. "He was slipping, not taking care of himself. I had to call him a couple times a day just to remind him to take his medication. The same thing with the agency. He wasn't on top of his game anymore."

"He tell you that?"

Richard leans in and pokes Jimmy in the chest. "I was worried about him. I called around. It didn't take much checking to find out."

Richard steps back and begins circling Jimmy.

"Not you," he says. "Me. You were never there. I was the one. And you think I can't look you in the eye?"

"Okay," Jimmy says. "Okay." He's watching his brother's hands.

"He needed something, I was the one who took care of it, Jimmy. Never you. He made excuses for you. I did what had to be done whether I wanted to or not. I looked out for him. And you, what did you do?"

Richard pauses, but keeps circling. "You. You can't even find the time to visit his goddamn grave. I had to identify the body, make all the arrangements. A closed casket, that's what they had to go with. No choice but that. You weren't there."

Richard abruptly stops. Jimmy braces, anticipating a swing, but Richard turns and walks back behind his desk. He glances up at the clock.

"Get out of here, Jimmy," he says. "Now.

FIVE

Evelyn Coates parks in the employee lot behind the Mesa branch of Frontier Cleaners. She's already forty-five minutes late for her stint on the afternoon shift. She drops her hand to the ignition key, but her fingers hesitate then move to her cell phone, where they punch in the number for the store, and she tells the manager, who's probably standing only a couple hundred feet away, that she's having car trouble and won't be in this afternoon.

She sits for a moment, revving the engine, then pulls back out of the lot, heading west on Baseline toward Phoenix until she hooks up with Route 87 and then cuts south, skimming the western boundary of Gilbert and straight-shooting it through Chandler.

Evelyn's tempted for a moment to get off on Warner or Ray Road and take either to where they intersect with McClintock and drive by the house where she was raised, but any impulse toward nostalgia feels false-bottomed, the Chandler she grew up in transformed beyond recognition now after Motorola, Intel, and Avent set up shop there and development went into overdrive, subdivision after subdivision filling the immense fields of cotton and soybeans that during her childhood had lain only a few blocks from her home. The chamber of commerce still touts the city's small-town charm, but for Evelyn it carries the metallic aftertaste of artificial sweetner.

Near Riggs Road, on the outskirts of town, she whips into the lot of a convenience store that's dressed up as a hacienda. She leaves the Mustang running and strides inside. A thin film of perspiration rides her hairline and neck, and she feels it lift from her skin in the arctic blast of air conditioning. She's the only customer in the store.

On impulse, imagining her husband's frown, Evelyn buys a single tallboy beer and then a lighter and a pack of cigarettes.

Back outside, she unsnaps and folds down the ragtop on the Mustang and gets behind the wheel again. She listens to the engine idling, feels its vibrations through the floorboard. She slips her hand beneath her skirt, catches the hem of her panties, and peels them down her legs and off, wadding and stuffing them in her purse before backing up and pulling out on 87 again.

Farther south the landscape begins to flatten and open up, mile upon mile of desert hardpan broken only by mesquite, creosote, and brittlebush, elephant trees, crucifixion thorn, and ironwood, lingering pockets of fading wildflowers, and scattered cacti standing like stranded chess pieces or misplaced coat racks.

Evelyn opens the tallboy and takes a long swallow. The wind rips through her hair, and the air streaming through the vents lifts and fills her skirt. She sets the beer between her legs. The inside of her thighs ripple in a long shudder when the can touches them.

She punches through the radio until she finds KZON. She wants something loud, harsh, and hormonal, songs stripped and raw, full of the blunt crazed grace of those too young to understand anything beyond what they feel.

She takes another swallow of beer. Rimming the far western horizon, the South Mountains and a couple of bumps beyond them, the Estrella Mountains, slowly recede every time she presses the gas, space begetting space, endlessly filling itself.

To the east a small dust storm churns and rises in the flat afternoon light.

The wind screams. She turns up the radio. She tries to remember the last time she heard her husband laugh.

He's a good man. He is. And she loves him. Evelyn just wishes she could remember something that had made him laugh, but she can't.

She pushes the Mustang through the flat, hard light. The condensation on the beer can trickles down the inside of her thighs.

Making a bet with herself, she drives with her eyes closed until the count of seven. Then on impulse counts out three more.

When she opens her eyes, she sees a jackrabbit flash through the underbrush.

She passes a stretch of blackened ground, the charred stumps of saguaro cacti that have become inadvertent lightning rods from the late spring storms.

She closes her eyes, counts again.

She's spent her life surrounded by good, decent men. Her father had been one. Everyone said so. He'd been a high school math teacher, and while her father may have found what he needed to negotiate his life in the truths governing quadratic equations and logarithms, he was totally helpless in the face of the everyday workings of the world. Her mother left when Evelyn turned twelve, and Evelyn stepped in and managed the household, doing all the cooking and cleaning, washing and ironing, the shopping and writing out of the monthly bills. She stayed at home, taking care of things, through high school and her first two years at Arizona State.

Where she met, fell in love with, and married Richard Coates.

Another good, decent man. Albeit a different one from her father.

Richard was passionate, at home in the world, full of plans. That's what had initially drawn her to him—his unwavering belief and confidence, lacking even a shred of arrogance, that he could accomplish whatever he set out to do. He knew how things worked. He was optimistic without being naive, principled and ambitious, fair in his treatment of others.

Evelyn dropped out of ASU at the close of her junior year. She'd been an art history major with secondhand plans that she'd borrowed from her best friend, Carol Findley, of working in one of the better art galleries in Scottsdale and maybe one day running one of her own.

At the time, though, Richard had gone into business with Charlie Wells and was scrambling to make it work. Money was tight and Evelyn wanted to help, so when the opening at Southwestern Airlines came up, she signed on as a flight attendant.

Richard went on to turn a haphazardly managed, barely break-even grounds maintenance service into a flourishing, lucrative operation. On the basis of his reputation for solid work and through long hours of canvassing, Richard had put the company in line for a number of long-term contracts with some of the larger resorts and retirement communities in Phoenix. Things were looking up. They bought a house in Encanto Park and eventually traded up to Scottsdale.

The house had a leviathan-sized mortgage that dwarfed the number of hours and whatever desire she had left for her degree, and Evelyn stayed on with Southwestern Airlines. With each takeoff, landing, and layover, the worlds of Rembrandt and Monet, Degas and Gauguin, shrunk and became convenient icebreakers for conversations at social gatherings and parties.

Then Richard discovered his partner had gone behind his back and set up a series of price-fixing schemes and rigged bids with their competitors. He'd also, without Richard's knowledge, begun hiring illegal aliens for some of the ground crew work. Charlie Wells refused to back down or change either of these practices when Richard confronted him, and Richard refused to work with anyone who condoned either one. They ended up dissolving the partnership. With the working capital he managed to salvage, Richard turned around and started Frontier Cleaners. Money again was tight, his hours long, and Evelyn this time left Southwest for United and a better salary and benefits package.

It didn't seem too much to ask. After all, Richard's plans were never just his plans; his plans were for them, the life they were building, the future they were building together.

The very future she now finds herself in but doesn't recognize. Or maybe recognizes all too clearly.

A life that has now come to feel like one of the morning paper crossword puzzles her husband likes to solve.

Something governed by definitions and whose fit and form only allow you to move in one of two directions.

Evelyn tears south, passing a white-on-green mileage sign for Coolidge. The sun's off to her right, a blazing yellow-white hole in the sky.

Under the right circumstances, decency, she thinks, becomes a burden.

Under the right circumstances, your plans, she thinks, begin to plan you.

Until one day, you find yourself sitting across from your husband and he says, *It's not too late. Thirty-nine's not too old. Lots of couples wait. You take care of yourself. You'd be a good mother.*

Your husband reaches across the table and takes your hand. *A new life,* he says.

What you feel, though, is the weight and shape of your own, how you've spent your entire life attending to the needs of others—your father's, your husband's, those of thousands of strangers on hundreds of flights—and you can't make your husband understand how the very idea of a child frightens you right now, a new life, a thumbnail of flesh that is pure unadulterated need, feeding on and growing inside you, a relentless presence you carry with you everywhere until it's ready to drop into your life wailing and grasping, all mouth and fingers, and you become the center of another cycle of need.

A family, a child, your husband says, *they make sense of things.*

But you don't want to make a child or sense right now.

You want to take off your panties and drive as fast as you can through the desert.

You want the flat, hard light, the wind, a landscape that promises nothing beyond itself.

Right now, you want the sun to burn you clean of everything, even decency.

But what you want more than anything else is simply this: to hear your husband laugh again.

SIX

Debt has a way of settling you in your skin.

So does the threat of death.

Jimmy dry-palms four aspirin and circles his room at the Mesa View Inn. It doesn't take long, the place a box with a narrow bathroom attached, a weekly rate stand-in for the idea of a home, cluttered with a lumpy bed, a couple of chairs, wall-paper whose fading design resembles underwear stains, a dresser with mismatched drawers, a portable black-and-white that picks up two stations, and a hot plate.

Traction, Jimmy thinks.

That's what he needs. A little traction.

After what happened between Richard and him, Jimmy moved to the next branch of the family tree and tried a long-distance call to Mom. She'd been divorced from the old man going on four years now, the marriage having sputtered along until Mom suddenly became a big fan of Jerusalem Slim, Mom cashing in her chips for a seat on the Hallelujah Express and three months after the divorce was finalized, landing a second husband in the same beat, a guy named Jerry Snapp, another born-again citizen, who owned two seafood restaurants in Tampa.

Mom was a regular sister of mercy now, big on religious homilies and quoting scripture passages, but decidedly tight with the maternal purse strings, so when Jimmy asked for the loan, he kept it simple, shaving away all references to Ray Harp and his collection practices and sticking to a tune he figured Mom might come in for the chorus on—the new-man, fresh-start melody—but she shut him down completely when it came to the cash, telling him how happy she was to hear he'd changed and how she'd always known he had the capacity to be more than he'd settled for and how it was important at this particular juncture in his life to trust in God to provide, and capping things off by saying that she and Jerry were praying for him.

The next thing, a dial tone. Jimmy had debated calling back and saying he appreciated all the prayers but maybe Mom and Jerry there, if they really wanted to do him some good, they could throw in another one, like Ray Harp maybe getting amnesia or eating it in a car wreck.

Traction.

One week.

He's even marked the date on the calendar, one of those complimentary jobs from his brother's business, Frontier Cleaners, Richard standing in front of the original store in Scottsdale, the addresses and phone numbers for the others listed below, then a bold-faced slogan: **We Clean What You Can't.** Jimmy had one of them hanging in his cell at Perryville, too.

Jimmy sits down on the edge of the bed. His hands are shaking, and he can feel the pulse in his neck take off.

He's been in jams before, but this thing with Ray Harp, it's got him worried.

He's wondering if maybe he's losing the touch. He's seen it happen. Plenty of other guys, their luck goes light and then just one day disappears. They keep doing what they've always been doing, but it just doesn't work anymore.

The Mesa View Inn, for example.

Jimmy's hit bottom a couple times, but he's never had to take up residence there.

Ditto with Perryville Correctional Facility.

One thing leading to another, that's the way Jimmy's used to playing it, and that's the way it's always worked ever since he washed out of his first semester at ASU for a little recreational pot-dealing among friends. That led to some new friends, and those friends had friends, and pretty soon Jimmy had lots of pals with interesting alternatives to regular employment.

Jimmy had the touch then, and though he told himself he'd know when to quit and take a French leave, it never quite happened. The world was full of sweet, easy deals, and he was going to live forever.

But then one day you blink and you're thirty-five, and one thing is not leading to another anymore. They're sprouting detours instead, none of which takes you where you want to go.

Jimmy gets up off the bed, circles the room, then ducks into the bathroom and splashes handful after handful of cold water on his face.

When he gets out, nothing's changed. He's still in the Mesa View Inn, and it's still the middle of the afternoon, and it still feels as if everything in the place is pointing a finger at him.

He bolts for the lot and points the pickup in the direction of the Chute.

On the way there, Jimmy works at striking a match on an idea to undo what his brother had done to him with the paperwork on the Dobbins parcel.

Nothing catches though. There's smoke but no spark.

Richard, though, had it all wrong about the grave and Jimmy not visiting it. He'd ducked going because he didn't want to have to stand at the foot of the plot and look at the marker and read his old man's name and the dates engraved on it, because that had a way of finalizing everything and Jimmy doesn't want to think of the old man that way, not yet. That's what he hates about cemeteries, the way they go about laying them out, everything designed and maintained to make one point: *it's over.*

And that's the one thing Jimmy doesn't want to think about when it comes to the old man.

Anything but over.

The old man had never missed visiting hours at Perryville Correctional. Not once. Jimmy knew he was a disappointment, but the thing was, the old man wasn't the type to point the finger. It just wasn't in him. It was a big world out there, and the old man knew the things it could do to you.

His whole life the old man had played it straight, never complaining, right up to the day his heart exploded on the way home from the insurance agency he ran, the old man having just made the entrance ramp to Route 10 when it happened, and he ended up plowing his car into the side of an eighteen-wheeler on the westbound.

Jimmy misses him, Jesus, he does.

Try explaining that to a tombstone though.

When he gets to the Chute, the place is quiet, the afternoon regulars just starting to show up. There are seven or eight scattered among the tables and a few more perched like dash ornaments at the bar.

Leon's tending, a sheet of newspaper spread flat in front of him with a fuselage of a model airplane in its center. Leon's got a long, crumpled tube of epoxy in one hand and a wing in the other when Jimmy sits down.

"A Zero," Leon says, nodding at the model. "Fast and to the point. The Nips knew aircraft."

Jimmy orders a draft and watches in dismay as Leon levers the handle.

Leon's a decorated air force vet with twenty missions over North Vietnam, but despite the legendary accuracy Leon has accorded himself in his war stories when it came to anything that passed between his crosshairs, Jimmy has never seen him draw a draft without leaving at least four inches of foam broiling below the lip of the glass.

Jimmy leans forward and squints at the shelf behind Leon. "Is that what I think it is?"

"Found it asleep in the jukebox," Leon says. "No telling how long it was there."

A couple of feet down from the cash register is a cracked aquarium patched with masking tape and topped by a piece of fine meshed screen held in place with a rock. In it is a fat sidewinder, its back alternately marked in brown and white dots the size of chocolate chips. Even in the bar light, the pattern of scales on its sides is as regularly defined as the tread on a new tire.

Leon flips a thick gray ponytail over his shoulder, then leans down and taps the glass with his index finger.

When the snake shifts its blunt wedge-shaped head and lifts its tail, Jimmy counts six rattles.

"That's some kinda mean," he says. "A real venom machine."

"Pass me the glue, will you, Jimmy?" Leon says before stepping over and tossing a small white mouse into the aquarium tank.

At around a foot and a half, the sidewinder takes up most of the floor of the tank. The mouse is on its hind legs, sniffing the air, its world shrunk to four square inches of loose dirt.

When the fangs hit, the mouse is flipped into the air. It flops around in the tank for a while. The snake, watching, slowly lowers its head, its jaws already starting to loosen and unhinge.

Jimmy hands Leon the glue. Leon starts to attach a miniature set of machine guns to the wing.

"Hey, don't talk to me about artificial intelligence," someone booms from the other end of the bar. "How do you feel about artificial beer? Same working principle. Artificial's artificial. It doesn't matter which way you try to slice the ham, Bill Gates ain't Solomon. No way."

Leon glances up, sighs, and shakes his head. "Tell you something, Jimmy. There's nothing more tiresome in this world as a drunk philosophy professor."

"Hey, Howie's all right," Jimmy says.

"Howard Modine is not all right," Leon says, setting down the wing. "The guy never shuts up. You think he's okay because he buys you drinks."

Modine walks over to where Jimmy's sitting and claps him on the back. He takes in the action in the cracked aquarium, the mouse half gone now, the closed eyes of the snake, the steady rhythm of jaws and throat.

"We must all suffer History," Modine says. His voice is deep and gravelly and always a couple of decibels louder than it needs to be, as if Howard works under the assumption that most of the people in the world have gone deaf.

"Even the snake," Howard adds. "The snake's not exempt."

Leon points across the room. "Take it to a table. I'm working here."

"Fine," Modine says. "Just how about bringing a few cold ones for my compadre, James Coates, the Cacti Bandit, and myself then?"

One night, near closing, Modine had heard the story about Jimmy's mishaps with the black-market saguaros and how that had landed him in Perryville Correctional, and Modine sent over a Lone Star on the house and they got to talking, though the conversation became lopsided, Jimmy doing most of the listening and signalling for more beers as Howard explained the shared underlying assumptions between the vagarities of the tenure review system at ASU and the venality and hypocrisy of the developers' landscaping practices.

Leon brings over some cold ones and quickly retreats behind the bar. Modine sets his attaché case in an empty chair, drops a stack of student papers to his left, and unwraps a fresh cigar. He's a small man with large features, a headful of tangled gray-brown hair and a bird's-nest beard.

"You're in early today," Jimmy says.

Howie explains that he's begun holding his afternoon office hours at the Chute. "The president wants more faculty involvement in the distance learning program," Howie continues. "It's his pet project. I'm doing my part to support it by putting as much distance as I can between my students and myself."

Modine parks the cigar in the ashtray and pulls the stack of papers closer. He glances over at Jimmy and uncaps a red pen. "I've seen you looking better, Compadre," he says.

Jimmy shrugs and takes a pull on the Lone Star.

"In fact, the way you look right now," Modine says, "I could probably use you as a visual aid for my Kierkegaard seminar. This week we're doing *Fear and Trembling.* "

Jimmy watches Modine put a red C-plus on the top paper and

then methodically work his way through the stack, putting the same grade on each, except for a couple he's separated and set to the side.

Modine recaps his pen and picks up his cigar. "The plus is for encouragement," he says. "Don't want to do any lasting damage to the self-esteem of the customers. You see, I don't have students anymore, James. I have customers. My job is to render unto Caesar and facilitate their needs so that what formerly was known as an education is now the equivalent of a Jiffy Lube for the soul."

Jimmy points his bottle in the direction of the small stack of unmarked papers and raises his eyebrows.

"I'm saving those for later, when I get home. Those I read and comment on. I'm blessed to have three or four unregenerates who are still laboring under the unfashionable assumption that a university is a place to explore ideas and enlarge the human spirit. Those papers are a reminder of why I got into this profession in the first place."

Howard pauses, quickly counts the number of dead soldiers on the table, and hollers to Leon to bring more reinforcements.

"You still haven't told me what's wrong," he says.

"In a nutshell, I'm more than a little short in the time and money departments."

"You need a loan?" Howard asks, pulling out his wallet. "I can spot you a couple twenties."

Jimmy waves him off. "I appreciate it, Howie, but we're talking Big, not Little, Picture here. And I'm running out of time."

"That's where we always find and lose ourselves," Howie says finally. "In Time. Always in Time." He scratches his head. "Our compadre Kirkegaard knew that. You take the leap of faith knowing that sooner or later it's going to become the long fall, because we're stuck in time and can't do anything about that, nothing. But for my money, the truth lies not in the leap or the fall, but precisely at the point where one becomes the other. That's where you want to set up shop."

"I'll keep that in mind," Jimmy says.

Forty-five minutes later, when Howard leaves for his evening class, Jimmy drifts over to the bar, and it's not long before Winston, owner of the Chute, steps up next to him.

"No tabs," Winston says, crossing his arms and nesting them on his chest.

Jimmy pantomimes deafness and waves him closer.

"No," Winston repeats, "tabs."

"Since when?"

"Since I checked the books and saw the one you ran up after first getting out of Perryville."

Winston's in his early fifties with a great sloping paunch avalanching against a pair of thick black suspenders and a wide round face that high blood pressure has shaded the color of wet bubble gum. There's a small, lumpy gray mustache hanging around his thick upper lip.

"I've also heard about your troubles with Ray Harp," Winston says. "No way I'm going to let a potential corpse stiff me."

"Okay, okay," Jimmy says, digging around in his jeans. He pulls out a crumpled wad of ones, all he has left from what he fenced out with Pete Samoa.

Winston leans over and fingers his way through the bills Jimmy's piled next to the ashtray. Jimmy can hear him counting to himself.

Winston steps back and tells Leon, "You shut him down when those are gone, understand?"

Someone calls Jimmy's name, and he turns and sees Don Ruger working his way through the tables, all smiles, his gait with a permanent hitch from a knee injury he got in one of the long string of auto accidents he's been in over the years.

"What's wrong with the forehead?" Jimmy asks when Don gets to the bar. "That's some kind of nasty."

Don grins sheepishly and lightly fingers the dark mass of bruise and contusion running from above his right eye to temple. Through its center is a vertical line of ragged homemade stitches.

"Got clotheslined by the Missus," Don says. "She had it strung across the front steps, knee-level, when I came home late from the track, you know, the one on Washington and thirty-eighth?" Don drops his hand and grins again. "Porch light was out, and I walked right into the line, went headfirst into the storm door. Glass everywhere after. I guess I should stay away from the dogs."

Don lightly punches Jimmy on the shoulder and winks, then turns to Winston when he notices that Winston hasn't moved off. "What's up?" he asks.

"What's up is whether you're going to pay up. I want to be sure you're more solvent than your pal there." Winston goes on to deliver the usual litany of complaint about Jimmy's overdue tab.

Don pulls out his wallet, then pauses. "You a betting man, Winston?"

Jimmy sees what's coming. "Not a good idea, Don. I'm a little rusty."

Don lays a hundred down on the bar. "Jimmy's tab against that. He'll do the Titties."

"I told you, I'm out of practice, Don. I don't think this is such a good idea." Jimmy's seen it before, Don wagering the weekly grocery money. Ditto with the green for the electric and water bills. "If we lose, Teresa will do more than clothesline you."

"I have faith in you," Don says. "I've seen you work."

Winston's looking at the hundred. "What do you mean, he'll do the Titties? What kind of bet is that?"

By now, word has started to snake through the bar, and a number of regulars have left their stools and tables and drifted over, standing in a clump behind Winston.

"Jimmy can give you fifty—" Don says, concentrating. "What you call them, Jimmy?"

"Synonyms," Jimmy says quietly.

"Yeah, okay," Don says. "Here's the deal. Jimmy can give you fifty synonyms for titties in a minute."

"No way," Winston says. "He can't. No one can. Not in a minute."

"I say yes." Don reaches up and lightly scratches at his stitches.

Jimmy shakes his head and sighs, but lets it ride.

Winston's fidgeting, his broad forehead sheened in a light sweat. He keeps tugging on his suspenders and then glancing at his watch. When he bites his lower lip, the slug of a mustache perched on his upper twitches and dips. Winston cranes his neck, looking around, taking in the crowd watching him, then resolutely dips into his pants pocket.

"Tell you what," he says. "Double or nothing."

"Don," Jimmy says, but he's waved off.

Don's nodding at Winston. "How about a little side bet, too? Five bucks for each one over fifty."

Winston takes off his wristwatch and sets it between Don Ruger and him. Then he pulls a small calculator from his shirt pocket and presses a couple buttons, clearing its face.

"You ready, Jimmy?" Don asks.

Jimmy looks at the door, but stays put. He nods.

"Ten seconds and counting," Winston says, looking down at the watch. "And it's fifty synonyms besides 'titties.' *Titties* don't count in the total." He smiles and points at Jimmy. "Go."

Jimmy leans back on the stool and aims his face at the ceiling, closing his eyes. "Silos. Jugs. Hooters. Tubes. Boomers. Torpedoes. Milk Steaks. Little Debbies. Melons. Rockets. Knockers. Bazooms. Saddle Bags. Paps. Milkshakes. Mammals. Jigglers. Snuggle Puppies. Headlights. Cushions. Squeegees. Pods. Balloons. Softies. Fixtures. Slope Heads. Tomatoes. Milk Duds. Meat Pies. Bags. Dynamic Duos. Hand-to-Mouths. Nipple Condos. Pillows. Tubes. Saucers. Chesties. Bouncers. Lamps. Dairy Products. Cha-Chas."

Winston's loudly marking time, trying to break Jimmy's rhythm. Jimmy, though, is in the zone, auctioneer-overdrive.

"Home stretch, Buddy," Don Ruger says.

"Full Moons. Dinner Plates. Tongue Twisters. Bra Babies. Three-Sixties. Bay Windows. Peaches. Sugar Bags. Badges. Butterballs. Twins. Hang Gliders. Plums. Knobs. Roundtables. Soft Touches. Chest Antlers. Cheese Keepers. Holy Rollers. Pies. Mommies. Peaks. Hat Racks. Front Lines. Handles. Ear Muffs.

Chubbies. Tourist Attractions. Safe Harbors. Grillwork. Sno-Cones. Tahitis."

"Seventy-three," Don Ruger says, slapping the bar top after Winston calls time.

Winston looks at Jimmy, picks up his watch, and then stalks off to his office. He's back in a few minutes with the money and Jimmy's tab, which he rips in two and drops on the floor.

Jimmy snaps his fingers. "Satellites," he says. "I forgot Satellites."

"Man," Don Ruger says, fingering his forehead. "I wish you'd been the dog running in the third at the track the other night. Would've saved me a whole lot of grief and green."

SEVEN

Frankie Coronado was the best jailhouse lawyer in the Perryville branch of the state of Arizona State Prison Complex, and Jimmy had driven out for early afternoon visiting hours and passed on two cartons of Camels and a couple bags of Almond Joys to Frankie and then the paperwork from his last meeting with Richard. Frankie took a distressingly short time looking over the stuff. There was also a lot of slow head-shaking.

"It's straight," he'd said finally.

"No holes?" Jimmy asked.

"None that matter." Frankie had gathered up his Camels and candy bars and raised his hand, signaling to the guard that the meeting was over.

Familia, he'd said, shaking his head one more time before he left.

A master plan, Jimmy is thinking on the drive back, that's what he needs. Not some scrawny, mewling runt of an idea, but a full-fledged master plan with all the accessories.

First, though, he has to make a quick detour to an Auto Zone for a quart of thirty-weight and some tranny fluid, replenishment for the beast he holds the pink slip on, which today, as usual, is burning one and leaking the other.

When he gets back on Route 10, Jimmy thinks he sees a flash of orange in the rearview, but it's not there when he checks a second time.

The sun's coming straight through the windshield and baking the cab of the truck. Jimmy had tried wedging a piece of cardboard into the skeleton of the visor, whose insides had dry-rotted away, but after a half hour of rattling and flapping, the cardboard had blown off and out the window.

Phase one of the master plan pretty much comes down to Jimmy trying to stay out of Ray Harp's way until he can come up with something that will net him some quick cash without landing him in Perryville Correctional again.

Phase two is finding some way to get his inheritance back or, barring that, making his brother pay one way or another for what he did.

Jimmy's still working on phase three.

When he checks the rearview this time, it's definitely there. A bright splash of orange.

It's there, and it's closing.

Jimmy, he knows how it's supposed to work. He's seen all the movies, the action flicks, the hero tailed by the bad guys, then suddenly kicking it in and rocketing out of there, the bad guys cranking it up, too, high-speed-pursuit time, lots of smoking and screeching tires, blaring car horns, sharp cornerings, narrow misses with buses and trucks, running red lights, civilian cars swerving and tipping over, the hero redlining it, the bad guys blasting away at him, Jimmy, like everyone else, able to summon up all the choreographed chaos and mayhem, the fancy stunt maneuvers and all their variations, until the hero either loses the bad guys through a stroke of daring and luck, or the bad guys screw it up and crash into something in a ball-of-flame finale.

Jimmy knows how it's supposed to work, but when he presses the gas, the Chevy starts shuddering, the transmission slipping into a long torturous whine before shifting up, and his breakaway move is a half-assed forty-seven miles per, barely two clicks above the minimum speed limit for Route 10. He glances in the mirror, hunches over the wheel, and keeps the truck pointed east.

The orange El Camino pulls into the space behind him. Newt Deems gives the horn a short tap.

Jimmy helplessly watches the 51st Avenue exit flip by. Even if he could run, he'd still have a hard time losing Deems. Not in Phoenix, he thinks. The streets in the city and every one of its subdivisions are laid out in a rigid right-angled grid. Eight hundred square miles of boxes. One, that's it, just one damn street in the whole town, Grant Avenue, that runs at a diagonal.

Newt Deems pulls the Camino into the left lane and even with Jimmy's pickup. Without looking at Jimmy, Newt hooks his hand over the roof and points at the sign for the next exit. Newt then punches the Camino into the right lane. Jimmy follows him down the ramp and a half block later into a dirt lot next to a roadside fruit-and-vegetable stand.

Newt Deems gets out and stretches, then walks over to the produce stand. Jimmy stays in the truck, trying to keep the engine at something approximating an idle, but it sputters and stalls out. Even with the windows open, the cab quickly fills with the smell of burnt oil.

Jimmy watches Newt approach. He's carrying a brown paper bag.

Everything about Newt suggests something that's been incorrectly assembled. He's a big guy, with overlapping and awkwardly proportioned slabs of muscle covering a squat torso. His eyes are set too close together, lost between the wedge of bone running straight across the base of his forehead and the thick bridge of his nose. He's sporting a long, thin bandito mustache and one of the most unfortunate haircuts Jimmy has ever seen on another human being—a seemingly impossible cross between a buzz and bowl cut.

You open a thesaurus, Jimmy thinks, and look up *gruesome,* you'd find Newt Deems listed as a synonym.

It's the meaty right hand that always gets to Jimmy though. Covering its back is a minutely detailed tattoo of a tarantula, its head and bared fangs perched on Newt's middle knuckles and its legs extending along the top of his fingers. Of the other three legs, one runs across the pad of flesh between thumb and index finger and down into his palm, and the other two curl over either side of his wrist.

Newt has this way of flexing his hand so that it looks like the spider's moving, the mouth even appearing to chew. The verisimilitude's kicked up a notch, too, by the fact that the back of Newt's hand is hairy.

Newt walks up to the truck and opens the door. Jimmy follows him over to the El Camino. Newt perches on the hood and pulls out a cell phone, punches in some numbers, and says, "I got him," and a moment later, "I wouldn't count on it." After giving directions, Newt slips the phone back into the breast pocket of a checked Western-cut shirt and opens the brown paper bag, taking out a nectarine.

Without taking his eyes off Jimmy, Deems unsheathes a buck knife and begins peeling the nectarine, his movements deft and practiced, the reddish-orange skin curling in one continuous piece no thicker than a postage stamp and dangling from the blade like a Mobius strip before Newt flicks it to the ground.

He holds up the nectarine. Its meat is wet and pulpy and glistens in the sunlight.

From where Jimmy's standing, the nectarine looks like a freshly dissected organ.

Newt pops it into his mouth whole and begins slowly chewing, pausing along the way to work the pit to the front of his mouth and catch it in his teeth before leaning over and spitting it into the dirt next to the right front tire.

Jimmy left his sunglasses in the truck, and the sun's cranking it up, the orange hood of the Camino starting to shimmer and ripple around Newt's bulk. Behind Jimmy is the insect drone of passing traffic.

Newt scratches the back of his wrist and watches Jimmy. After a while he slides off the hood and wipes his hands on his jeans. "There we go," he says, walking over to a blinding-white Continental that has stopped in the middle of the hard-packed dirt fronting the produce stand. Newt opens the rear passenger door and ushers Jimmy inside.

Ray Harp glances over, then returns his attention to the woman sitting in a modified fold-down jumpseat across from him. There's a small tray in front of her. She's working on Ray's nails.

The driver pulls out of the lot and heads east and then south.

Jimmy cranes his neck and looks out the rear windshield. The El Camino's following them.

"Get me a beer, will you, Jimmy?" Ray nods toward a small white ice chest on the seat between them. Ray's got the Allman Brothers going on the CD player.

Jimmy cracks a cold one and hands it over. He hesitates, waiting for Ray to offer him one, but it's snake-eyes on that idea, so Jimmy replaces the lid and watches Ray drain the beer in one long swallow.

You can't take the biker out of the businessman, Jimmy thinks. Ray's in his mid-forties with thick salt-and-pepper hair fanning over his shoulders. He's wearing a metallic blue three-piece suit but no shirt and a pair of needle-nosed ostrich-skin cowboy boots.

Ray's the kind of guy who could make Darwin blush—an ex-biker with just enough smarts, luck, and muscle to oversee a significant cut of the crank trade in Phoenix and the surrounding region, Ray organizing the biker gangs into a loose confederation and then franchising the action, going on to clean up the labs, too, shutting down the half-assed amateur operations, upgrading equipment and coordinating the distribution of chemicals, establishing something approaching quality control for the product and thus keeping the prices regulated, Ray then buttressing his power base by working out some admittedly shaky but still mutually beneficial live-and-let-live deals with some of the more vicious Mexican crank gangs and going on to buy up enough local and state law enforcement officials to keep things running.

The driver keeps the Continental pointed south. They cross Baseline, headed toward the South Mountains, sticking to back roads. They pass weathered trailers up on blocks, run-down stucco and adobe farmhouses, faded tract homes set on bare lots, the space between things slowly opening up, the landscape bisected by the spine of the Western Canal system. In the distance, puncturing the skyline above the mountains is a tall crosshatched cluster of radio and television towers.

The woman shapes and rounds Ray's nails into perfect crescents. Her head's bent, the wall of straight black hair hiding most of her face. She's wearing a shiny green miniskirt that looks like it's made of plastic and a pink-and-white-striped elastic tube top. Above it is a thin silver necklace with dangling pendants of the four phases of the moon. Her nails are the color of new dimes.

"Crazy weather, huh, Jimmy?" Ray says, gesturing out the window. "Here it is, June already, and it's like everything's out of balance. One week spring, the next summer, then back again. No middle ground."

Ray drops the empty on the floor of the Continental. "You look outside and then at the calendar, you can't make them match. You notice that, Jimmy?"

"Now that you mention it," Jimmy says.

"I was wondering if maybe that was the problem," Ray says, "why you keep forgetting to pay me. You know, if the weather's got you confused. As of today, you're past due for the third time."

Jimmy takes it slow, laying out the details for Ray, keeping their sequence straight, starting with his plan to get the taxes on the parcel paid but then detouring into some R&R with Marci, the waitress who eventually introduced him to the friend of her brother who worked at America West with the Suns and had the inside dope on Penny Hardaway's injury, Jimmy's bet on the point spread against the Lakers, the bet backfiring on him, Jimmy taking the job at Big and Bigger Jones's Old Wild West Park and getting fired, Jimmy regrouping, deciding to swallow his pride and ask his brother for a loan to pay off the back taxes on the Dobbins parcel, Jimmy figuring he could then put the place up for collateral and secure a loan that would let him pay off what he owed Ray, and that all disappearing when his brother pulled his fine-print power of attorney number with the paperwork on the place, Jimmy right back where he started when he got out of Perryville and went to Ray in the first place.

After Jimmy's finished, Ray's quiet for a long time, appearing to think over what he's heard. The woman remains bent over Ray's left hand, her movements small and delicate as she works on each nail. In the background is Duane Allman's doomed voice.

With his free hand, Ray raids the cooler for another beer. "Ninety percent of business," he says, "is image. People believe what they think they see." Ray pauses to crack open the beer. "Take the Mex crank gangs, for example. Took me a long time to work out the agreements, get them to trust me and work together. Everyone's making money, but still they're suspicious of each other—of me, too. It's the nature of things. Something like trust, it's very fragile and complicated. That's where image comes in. You got to make people believe what they think they see. Otherwise you're tomorrow's lunch." Ray pauses again and looks at Jimmy over the top of his beer. "I don't intend to be on anyone's menu, Jimmy."

Jimmy reassures Ray that he's not interested in becoming an entree either.

A couple seconds later, Jimmy realizes they're on Dobbins Road. He starts waving his arms. "Ray, up there in a little bit, on your right, that's what I was telling you about, my grandfather's property. Twenty acres. I don't have to point out the development potential to you. Like I said, the city's moving south. It doesn't have anywhere else to go."

The farmhouse is a faded brown stucco a couple hundred yards off the road. It sits on a flattened crest of a long, irregularly inclined slope dense with overgrown interlocking thickets of mesquite and brush. There's no other house for a half mile on either side of it.

Jimmy yells, "Hey, I said slow down, okay?" He glances up and catches the driver's eyes in the rearview.

Oh shit, Jimmy thinks.

No one who's ever met Aaron Limbe forgets the eyes. They're the palest of gray and empty, absolutely empty. No life in them at all. None. Zombie peepers.

"Heard about your old man," Limbe says, waiting a couple beats before adding, "I'm glad he's dead."

"Aaron's two-fisted when it comes to holding a grudge," Ray says. "He wanted to kill you the first tick past the repayment deadline."

Again, the blank eyes in the rearview. Jimmy looks away, at the back of Limbe's head, the sharp square lines of his haircut, the tendons on either side of his neck corded like twin stalks of broccoli.

Aaron Limbe's grudge came down to this: He blamed Jimmy for getting him kicked off the Phoenix police force. That might have been technically true, but it hadn't been personal on Jimmy's part. Expedient, yes, since Jimmy had been in some tight circumstances at the time.

He'd just been nicked for grand theft auto and ended up making a deal with the police commissioner to get the charges dropped in exchange for info that directly implicated Limbe in a politically charged case involving the murder of a prominent Mexican American attorney and twelve illegal aliens.

It wasn't like Aaron Limbe didn't deserve what happened to him. As far as Jimmy was concerned, Limbe was the worst breed of cop. Not corrupt, but bent, badly bent.

The thing Jimmy had never counted on was Aaron Limbe finding out that it had been Jimmy who snitched him out. In addition to dropping the grand theft charges, the commissioner had promised Jimmy anonymity for anything he brought to the table.

Somehow Aaron Limbe had found him out. It had taken awhile, but he had.

By that time, Jimmy had been popped for the black-market saguaros.

Limbe had shown up twice at Perryville Correctional during

visiting hours. Jimmy had been afraid he was going to go Jack Ruby on him, but he made no reference to the case involving Ramon Delgado or the twelve dead Mexican Americans. All Limbe did was watch him with those dead eyes and utter a single sentence each time before he left.

No mercy, he'd said.

That's it. Nothing more.

Then Aaron Limbe dropped out of sight.

Jimmy had heard rumors he'd left the state and hooked up with one of those fringe militia groups. He hadn't expected Limbe turning up working for Ray Harp.

The woman gathers her instruments and folds up the tray, her hair falling away when she sits back in the jumpseat and takes the beer Ray offers her.

Her green plastic skirt crackles when she crosses her legs. Jimmy gets his first look at her. She's not the biker chick he'd earlier assumed. She's a Native American. More than likely a Paiute.

"Is there going to be much blood with this one?" she asks, opening the beer. Her voice has the flat tones of a telephone recording.

Ray Harp leans over and turns up the Allman Brothers.

They leave Dobbins and head farther south into a stretch of no-man's-land between the South and Estrella Mountains, a little side trip into a landscape that's full of dry washes and lunar outcroppings of rock, the vegetation completely feral, stunted and twisted in some places, tangled and overgrown in others.

Aaron Limbe taps the brakes and takes a left onto the ghost of a dirt road. Newt Deems follows in the Camino. They're headed in the direction of the Gila River.

The road dips and twists and then unexpectedly opens onto a large clearing of flat hardpan ringed in boulder-strewn rubble and creosote bushes.

"Okay," Ray Harp says.

Limbe parks the car and throws the trunk latch. Jimmy watches Newt and him take out a folding table and a large beach umbrella. They unfold and set up both a few yards from the car, then return for a wicker picnic basket and the cooler in the back seat. Newt goes back to the trunk for some folding lawn chairs. Limbe carries a square black box and sets it on the hood of the Continental.

"Ray, I'll get you the money," Jimmy says. "Gospel. I just need a little more time."

Ray and the woman get out of the car and walk over to the beach umbrella and table and sit down.

Newt Deems pulls Jimmy out of the car and ties his hands behind his back with a piece of nylon rope.

Aaron Limbe comes over, a black strip dangling from his hand, and fastens it around Jimmy's neck. In his other hand is a remote control.

Limbe reaches over and touches something beneath Jimmy's chin. There's a click, then a series of short, low, evenly spaced beeps.

Limbe snaps his fingers and Newt takes Jimmy by the elbow and leads him a good thirty yards out in the desert, then turns and walks back to join the others.

Jimmy's standing out there, fronting the table.

Aaron Limbe hands Ray the remote. The dark-haired woman begins passing out sandwiches and beer.

Ray points the remote control at Jimmy.

"It only takes one," he says. "Just one deadbeat to put the wrong signals in the air and pretty soon everyone's tuned to the frequency, all of them thinking, 'Ray's not on top of his game anymore. He's getting soft.' The next thing I know, I'm looking at a groundswell movement. The Mexicans, nobody has to take Ray Harp seriously anymore. Just ask Jimmy Coates."

The sun's tattooing Jimmy's head pore by pore. The thing below his chin is softly humming, like the sound a refrigerator makes late at night when you hear it from another room.

A cloud of yellow and white butterflies whirls past. His shadow looks like it's painted on the hard-packed earth. A swarm of red ants roils at the base of a stunted yucca a couple feet to his right. His throat feels funny, a slight but persistent tickle spreading upward from its base.

Jimmy's ears suddenly pop, and he's knocked to his knees.

He gets up, and a couple seconds later the same thing happens. The fingers of his bound hands begin to twitch.

Jimmy backs off, but gets no further than a couple of steps before the air implodes. His breath is torn from him. His insides squeezed. He's back on his feet, but barely.

"What the hell?" he yells, but doesn't recognize his voice. It's raspy and dislocated, like a bad ventriloquist's trick.

He looks down. He's standing in the swarm of red ants. The inside of his mouth tastes singed. His ears pop and buzz. He's sweated through his clothes.

"What the hell?" he says again.

Ray waves to him from under the umbrella and calls out, " Did Aaron ever tell you he'd done some Special Forces work down in Nicaragua and Honduras before he joined the police?" Ray pauses to take a bite of his sandwich. "Those Special Forces guys, they're a pretty resourceful bunch. They'll take something basic, like one of those electroconvulsive dog collars, say, and modify it so that it can be put to any number of interesting new uses."

Ray hands the remote to Limbe and goes back to his sandwich. Next to him, the woman palms and tilts a compact and readjusts the lines of her lipstick.

Jimmy takes three steps back, and he's off his feet again. It feels like someone's taken a hammer to his spine. He rolls around in the dirt for a while.

Then he's on his feet and running. West. Toward the Estrella Mountains. Away from them all. The ground keeps shifting under his feet and he's dizzy and it's hard to maintain his balance because his hands are tied behind his back, but he's doing the only thing that makes sense: running.

This time it's insects.

He feels like a dense roiling swarm of bees has replaced his skin, and they're clustered on and crawling over his nerve endings.

Jimmy's lying flat on his back with the sun in his eyes. It takes a long time to get back on his feet.

He's conscious of the dog collar and of each step he takes now. He braces himself, trying to anticipate the moment when space and light will collapse into pain, but he's walking blind, no idea anymore how long he's been out there, the heat squeezing him, reference points starting to melt, the landscape hiding from itself, a snake catching ahold of, then methodically swallowing, its tail, the twisted yucca and creosote around him losing definition, thin lines now, like stray pencil marks against the light, Jimmy moving carefully across the hardpan, sweat in his eyes, muscles jumping, everything in the landscape fleeing or melting or shrinking except Jimmy, who's stuck in his skin.

They're watching him from under the umbrella, all of them except Newt Deems, who's standing off to the side and flipping his buck knife into the air, where it disappears into the light and then magically reappears in his hand.

Aaron Limbe raises his arm, levels it at Jimmy.

Jimmy stops, hesitates, then takes another step.

This time it's like getting thrown through a windshield.

Jimmy's breathing glass, choking on it, flailing about on the ground, trying to find his center of gravity and get upright again.

His right cheek is scraped raw from the fall, and his vision's distorted, eyes almost swollen shut, thin slits now, full of dirt and sweat.

He's reduced to a howl of outrage and pain. A howl intended to fill hundreds of square miles of desert and bring the sky down. A raw, protracted howl that comes from some place deep inside him that Jimmy never knew existed.

He senses movement, that Ray and the others have moved closer, and still howling, he rushes them.

Space and light refuse to yield. He's knocked down over and over again.

He hears Aaron Limbe saying something about doing judgments.

Jimmy's eyes have swollen shut.

He staggers in wide, sloppy circles, the howl having leaked away into a dry rasp.

He stumbles, stops to regain his balance, and then the ground is pulled out from under him.

Ray Harp's voice searches him out. It seems to come from all directions at once.

"You ever have a pet, Jimmy?"

The insides of his eyelids are burning. His body feels like pain has moved from rental to homeowner status.

"I asked you a question, Jimmy. Did you ever have a pet?"

Jimmy croaks out an affirmative.

"I thought so." Ray's voice is disembodied and cloudy. "I bet it was a dog, right? A mongrel, one of those loveable mutts, a United Nations of breeds, a little of this and that, we're establishing the dog's cute and adorable, a boy's best friend, right?"

When Jimmy nods, the pain simultaneously runs the length and width of his body.

"I figured so. We got this established then. You had your basic mongrel, a loveable pet, but we still don't know his name."

"Trevor," Jimmy rasps.

Aaron Limbe's voice barrels down. "That's a real asshole name, Trevor."

"My brother named him," Jimmy says.

"Well, we're making headway here," Ray says. "We have Trevor, and he's a loveable mutt. A regular part of the family. Jimmy and his brother's boyhood companion." Ray's voice disappears for a moment. "I'm betting your brother named the dog, but you saw him as yours. I'm also betting Trevor, as adorable as he was, was also what we'd call 'spirited.' Too much energy for his own good, had a hard time following commands, got into some scrapes around the neighborhood, am I right? Chasing cats, digging up flowers, barking all night, leaving dumps in people's front lawns, maybe growling and nipping at the mailman. Would it be fair to say, Jimmy, that Trevor had a reputation for doing things that caused trouble for himself and others?"

Jimmy's hands and wrists are going numb, and the sun's in his face, but when he tries to shift position and roll onto his side, Ray puts his boot on Jimmy's chest and pins him where he lies.

"Now I'm sure," Ray says, "you worked with Trevor. You didn't want to see him get in any more trouble. You disciplined him, right? Made sure he understood what he was and was not supposed to do. You established some rules and guidelines, I'm saying, correct? All designed to protect Trevor from his own worst impulses. Trevor, of course, wants to please you. He tries. But it's just not in him. He's spirited. He can't help himself. He crosses the line, and the next thing you know, Trevor has no use for oxygen anymore. One of the neighbors, they shoot him or stop by the house and lay it out for your old man and he shoots him, or the neighbor, he calls the pound and they pick Trevor up." Ray pauses, then asks, "Am I close on my take here, Jimmy?"

The pressure of Ray's boot on his sternum makes Jimmy start coughing. Until it subsides, he's afraid his bones are going to fly apart.

"What finally happened to Trevor?" Ray asks.

"He got run over by a car," Jimmy eventually gets out. "Trevor liked to bite tires."

"Nothing pretty about a squashed dog," Ray says. "You bury him, Jimmy?"

"No. My brother did."

"That's good," Ray says and leans down so that his voice seems to touch Jimmy's face. "Then he's used to it, in case he has to do it again. Because you got one week to get the cash you owe me. One week." Ray pauses for a moment. "We clear on that, Jimmy? Otherwise, you'll get the chance to see how resourceful Aaron Limbe can be with some vise grips and a soldering gun."

EIGHT

"You were fine," Evelyn tells her husband, lightly placing her hand on his chest. "Relax, okay?"

A part of her listens for any false bottoms to her words, because the truth is he was less than fine tonight, their coupling never quite in sync, Evelyn struggling to meet and match his rhythm, and by the time she'd adjusted, feeling a small welling start deep inside her, Richard had already finished, his orgasm tearing a low groan from him, just before he dropped his face into the pillow. A few moments later, he pulled out and rolled over on his back.

"It's just that things have been kind of tense lately," he says as his breathing evens. "I've had a lot on my mind. And tonight didn't make anything better with Jimmy showing up out of the blue."

"Like I said, relax. It's not like I was timing you." Though that, too, was not strictly true. Evelyn had looked over at the clock.

For most of their marriage, Evelyn had no real complaints about their lovemaking. Richard was a patient lover, methodical and attentive, skillful if not as passionate as Evelyn sometimes hoped for, but true to course, both of them early on in the marriage having discovered the basic elements of what gave each other pleasure and staying with them. There may have been few surprises between the sheets, but there were equally few disappointments also.

Evelyn had been looking forward to having more time together after she quit the airlines, but everything in their lives had quietly shifted off center after her father-in-law died. With Richard, the dynamics of their lovemaking turned lopsided. Its frequency increased but became increasingly shadowed by something else, a small rift, Richard not quite there even while he moved between her legs, Evelyn sensing it even in his kisses, something purposeful and resolute channeled into affection and attraction, as if even his own pleasure had become secondary, subordinated to the importance of delivering sperm.

Because that's finally what drifted between them, shadowing them both in and out of bed—Richard's desire for a child. He saw starting a family in the same terms as starting a new business. You made plans and put those plans into action. You applied yourself. You stuck to your goal. You made things work.

It's not that simple, Evelyn wants to tell him, but she can't. He can't or won't talk about his father, and she can't or won't tell Richard that she's continued to get her birth control prescription filled.

It should be simple. After all, they know each other better than anyone else. They've made a good life together. They should be able to talk things through. They're two rational and sensible adults.

Except Evelyn's also discovered something. She's finding it easier and easier to lie. Each lie is like opening a window. She's not sure if she's letting something in or out, and for now she's not sure it matters.

Richard rolls over, presses his lips lightly on hers, and gets out of bed. It's the beginning of another ritual she's accustomed herself to over the years: Richard's postcoital shower.

Tonight, though, he hesitates, standing naked by her side of the bed, and Evelyn gives him a smile, pursing her lips, a little test run to perhaps getting him back in bed for another try. She still feels the faintest outline of the orgasm she was headed toward earlier.

"He's got to learn to help himself," Richard says. "There are limits. Everything has limits. Even forgiveness. Maybe especially forgiveness. Jimmy still has to learn that. He would have lost the farm unless I stepped in. I did what I had to. That's never easy."

Evelyn can still hear it: the long lean on the doorbell. She and Richard had been out back on the deck, Richard grilling salmon steaks, so she had answered the door and found her brother-in-law on the front steps, looking like he'd been mauled, Jimmy unshaven, in dirt-stained jeans and a beat-up Phoenix Suns T-shirt ripped along the seam of the right shoulder, a tuft of hair poking through, his skin blotchy and red and his eyes almost swollen shut. He'd stumbled past her into the house, saying over and over in a raspy voice that he needed to talk to Richard.

Richard had closed the sliding glass doors to the deck, and Evelyn had stood in the kitchen with her glass of white wine, overhearing snatches of conversation.

I'm begging you, Richard.

Never change. Your own good.

I'm jammed.

Has to stop sometime.

Don't understand. What they did and what they'll do if.

Dad's problem, he didn't.

Will you listen to.

Same thing. All your life.

Evelyn hears the shower going, and Richard talks as he adjusts the water temperature. "What's right is never easy. Nobody seems to understand that anymore, Evelyn."

Her hand has drifted down over her stomach. She closes her eyes. She bows her legs so that her feet are touching, sole to sole. The water drums the shower walls, shrouding her husband's voice. Evelyn moves her fingers through her pubic hair. Her breath catches as she finds herself.

NINE

The master plan's up and running except for when Jimmy puts in a call to Don Ruger, and Teresa, Don's wife, picks up, and as soon as she hears Jimmy's voice, immediately hangs up.

Call number two. Ditto.

On the third, Jimmy says as quickly as he can, "Come on, Teresa. Let me talk to Don."

A little hesitation and enough silence for Jimmy to lever in with, "Otherwise I'll have to come over there. I really need to talk to him."

Teresa bangs down the receiver hard, but the connection's open. Thirty seconds later, Don's on the line. Jimmy can hear Teresa in the background bringing down a bilingual string of curses upon his head.

Jimmy doesn't waste any time. "I got something lined up, Don. Something solid."

Don clears his throat a couple of times.

"Did you hear what I said? I got a job I could use some help on."

More silence and throat-clearing backdropped by Teresa's wrath.

"Is there a problem?" Jimmy asks. "I mean, besides Teresa's ongoing desire to castrate me?"

Jimmy figures the guy who climbed Mount Everest, that was

tying shoes compared to trying to get on Teresa's good side. In her eyes, Jimmy was a direct emissary of El Diablo, and whose sole purpose was to devise ways to lead her husband astray. No way Jimmy's ever going to change the color on that picture. Teresa's first generation, but the family taproots are still in south Mexico, and she's a starter for the Pope's team.

"When you planning to do it?" Don asks finally.

"Today."

"Oh man. Today? The thing is, I gotta hang a couple ceiling fans, and then I promised the kids I'd take them to the Hall of Flame museum, look at all the fire-fighting stuff."

"Excuse me," Jimmy says. "I must have the wrong number. I thought I was talking to Don Ruger, this guy I know who the other night at the Chute was begging, practically hands and knees, the guy begging to be let in if something came up on account of this guy is going crazy punching the clock at Renzler's Meats and watching his paycheck go up in Pampers and having to do stuff like hang ceiling fans. This guy, Don Ruger, was looking for a little supplemental income, no withholdings, and enough action, get the juices flowing again, to remind him that there's more to life than cutting rump roasts and going to eight o'clock Mass and doing ring around the rosary."

"Oh man," Don says again. "It's just that I ran into Pete Samoa yesterday, and Pete was saying it might not be a good idea—even though you're my friend and all, Jimmy—to hang out with you right now. Pete's hearing that Ray Harp's plenty pissed at you and that'll extend to anyone in the vicinity."

Jimmy sighs. "Don, what do you think the point of this job is? I'm going to use my cut to settle with Ray. Ray's not interested in you. Besides, he'll never have to know you were in on it. You're clear as far as that's concerned."

"Maybe," Don says. "It's today, you said?"

"This afternoon. We need the morning to get organized, set things up. Are you in or not?"

"I guess so, yeah."

"You're in, we're moving. I'm at the Mesa View. Get over here as soon as you can. If Teresa says anything, tell her you got to take me to the doctor, and they'll probably have to run some kind of tests afterward."

"What for?"

"Who cares? Tell her anything. She'll be happy enough just to hear I'm sick." Jimmy pauses, about to hang up. "Oh, I almost forgot. Bring your ATM card. We're going to need some up-front money."

"You didn't say anything about front money before."

"I know. I just said I almost forgot. That means I didn't think of it until now."

"How much you talking about?"

"Four Bens."

Don's back to the throat-clearing routine. Either that or the line's sprouted some serious static.

"It's a stake, Don," Jimmy says, unsuccessfully keeping the impatience from his voice. "Christ sake, this job's a cherry. You'll get the front money back before we do the split. The thing is, if you're in, we need to get moving. I'm talking both-feet commitment."

"Okay, okay," Don says. "I'll see you in a half hour."

Jimmy then puts in a call to Pete Samoa for two pistols, Jimmy explaining no heavy artillery, just something that makes a simple statement, a Smith & Wesson nine-millimeter, say, or a Colt Cobra, Pete of course bitching about the short notice, Jimmy for his part bitching about Pete's prices, but the thing's in motion by the time he hangs up.

Don's outside the Mesa View in his yellow Aries, and Jimmy hops into the passenger seat, and they head for Baseline, driving west until they spot an ATM, Don extracting the four Franklins, his feet wet now and his mood improving. He's nodding his head and grinning. Jimmy turns on the radio, catches his favorite oldie, Van Morrison growling his way through "Gloria," and that just sweetens the pot.

"I got to tell you," Don says when they're back on Baseline. "After I hung up talking to you, I unpacked one of those ceiling fans. I still wasn't sure, you know, and I thought maybe it wouldn't be so bad, me doing something regular around the house, helpful regular stuff, you know; but then I'm looking at this clump of wires, and the instructions are in three languages, and Manny's got the cartoons blaring and Nina's crying and Gabriel and Gabriella are playing around in the toolbox, and I'm trying to figure out what color wire is the ground, and then I'm just looking at the picture of the ceiling fan on the box, the thing, it's hanging down from a bunch of white puffy clouds, lots of blue sky around, and the next thing I know, I'm in the Aries on my way to the Mesa View."

"The Big Itch," Jimmy says. "It's there, you got to scratch it. That's what fingers are for."

They hit a strip mall anchored by a Target. Jimmy likes the store's logo, that red bull's-eye. They buy a package of thin latex gloves, two canvas bags, some allergy masks, a couple of baseball caps, two pairs of wraparounds, and a large blue bandana that Don can twist headband-style to cover the bruises and stitches on his forehead from getting clotheslined on the front steps of his house by Teresa when he'd come in late from the dog track.

"Some different wheels," Jimmy says. "That's what we need now." Don backtracks, going east on Baseline, to a place Jimmy noticed on the way in, Westfield Automotive, a bread-and-butter repair shop sandwiched between a Wendy's and a florist's.

If Jimmy's going to boost a car, he'd just as soon avoid messing with the mechanics of the new antitheft devices or scouting row after row in a mall parking lot for a careless shopper.

He tells Don to park a couple of slots down from the entrance, out of sight of the doors, and Jimmy gets out and saunters in.

The woman behind the counter is in her early fifties with some mortuary-quality makeup. Nothing in her face moves when she smiles and asks what Westfield Automotive can do for him. Her hair is a shade of brown a decade behind her eyes.

Jimmy tells her he has a sick pickup and he's shopping around, looking for a rebuilt engine.

The woman nods and says she'll get Mac. He's the one Jimmy needs to talk to.

As soon as she leaves, Jimmy scans the wall to the right of the cash register. It's full of invoices and dangling car keys. Jimmy spots an Acura he likes and grabs the paper and keys, stuffing them in the front pocket of his jeans.

Then he stands at the counter and discusses the availability of rebuilt engines with Mac and says he'll get back with him soon.

Jimmy exits Westfield Automotive and heads for the gravel lot behind the shop, spotting the gold Acura in the second row and nodding to a mechanic taking a cig break at a back bay, Jimmy pulling out the invoice and keys and walking over to the car. He gets in and fires it up.

He drives back to the Target parking lot. Don Ruger shows up a few minutes later. He takes the essentials from the Aries and moves them to the Acura.

They're off, Jimmy checking the dash clock and seeing they're ahead of schedule, then cranking up the air in the Acura, chasing down a decent radio station, hitting a drive-through for a couple of sodas, and heading north toward Pete Samoa's.

It's a fine day, the sky a soft blue, sweet as an open billfold, temp in the low nineties, Jimmy feeling it, that point where luck turns a corner and it's all systems go. There's not a cloud in sight for at least one hundred miles.

The radio's playing the Stones.

Pete has the goods ready. An Astra Constable .32 for Don, a Charter Arms Pathfinder for Jimmy. Pete tells them both handguns have been around the block a few times so it'd be a good idea to wear gloves and dump both guns the same day.

Jimmy takes Route 10 to the Hohokam Expressway then north to Scottsdale. Jimmy hangs a right on Chaparral Road. He's thinking about two nights ago, going to his brother for help, Jimmy hating the memory of the pure need in his voice, the unabashed begging that Ray Harp's ultimatum after their little session in the desert had reduced him to, Jimmy hating that need in his voice even more than he hates Richard refusing to listen and shutting him down.

The sound of yourself begging, no one should have to hear that.

So you start at the beginning. That's the plan, Jimmy tells himself. *You start at the beginning.*

A half mile down Chaparral, Jimmy pulls into the lot for a video store. Less than a block away are the sign and logo—a two-armed saguaro crested by a bright yellow sun—for Frontier Cleaners. It's the one featured on the calendar, the first of the seven stores in his brother's chain.

Jimmy runs through the moves one more time for Don Ruger. The Acura in the employee parking lot, out back. Usually seven people per store, five with the machines, a manager roaming, a cashier. Don going in the rear door, herding the employees into the break room. Jimmy through the front, locking the doors, taking the cashier, Don watching the manager until he or she opens the safe, then moving the manager and cashier to the break room, locking all of them in. Jimmy cutting the phones. Don and Jimmy leaving through the back door.

Simple and straightforward, that's the ticket. Minimum surprises. Jimmy knowing the layout of the store and the workstations from his short stint delivering for Frontier after his brother locked down a contract with a nursing home franchise. As far as jobs went, it wasn't too bad, Jimmy getting to know a couple of the RNs at the homes who knew some fun ways to compensate for an eight-hour face-to-face with mortality, Richard constantly on Jimmy's back about being on time and having to let him go in another object lesson for Jimmy's own good.

Jimmy's smiling now, though, getting out of the driver's and moving to the passenger seat, putting on the baseball cap and sunglasses, looping the allergy mask around his neck, tucking the Charter Arms in the waistband of his jeans and pulling the Phoenix Suns T-shirt over it. The canvas bag is between his feet. He's ready.

They wait until there's a break in customer traffic, then Jimmy's out and through the front doors, locking them, flipping over the CLOSED sign, and pulling down the blinds before the cashier registers what the sequence is leading to. Jimmy can hear Don in back, rounding up employees.

Jimmy drops the canvas bag on the counter and points toward the register. He has his right arm bent, the Charter Arms pointing at the ceiling.

"Everything," he says.

"The coins, too?" the cashier asks.

"I said everything, didn't I?" Jimmy thinking this is more than a holdup. It's a little object lesson for Richard as well.

Everything.

Don walks the manager up and takes over watching the cashier while Jimmy moves the manager to his office and the safe. The manager's a dapper silver-haired guy, starched white shirt and conservative tie, who has the irritating habit of repeatedly pointing out the obvious.

"This is wrong," he says over and over. "Wrong, I'm telling you. To come in here and do this, it's not right. Criminal activity is wrong. This is a respectable business. We've never been robbed before. This is not right, what you're doing. There's no way you can pretend otherwise. It's simply not right."

Jimmy finally has to give the guy a close-up of the Pathfinder to get him going on the safe.

When they're done, Don locks the manager and cashier in the break room with the others. Jimmy cuts the phone lines.

They're out in less than seventeen minutes.

Jimmy tells Don to take Hayden Road north toward Frank Lloyd Wright Boulevard.

Jimmy sets the canvas bag on the floor. Don drives them through Old Scottsdale. He's a driver's-ed teacher's dream—no speeding, Mr. Rules of the Road.

The deejay on the radio is everybody's friend.

Even with the car windows closed, Scottsdale smells of money. Every blade of grass has a price tag.

Just past the municipal airport is Frontier Cleaners store number two.

Jimmy and Don are on the clock, straight autopilot. They have the moves down. The store's a walk-through.

They're out in just under fifteen minutes.

Then it's a backtrack, Jimmy keeping Squaw Peak in sight, navigating, Don taking Thunderbird Road to Tatum Boulevard and south to Doubletree Ranch, and they're in Paradise Valley now, Jimmy keeping an eye on the clock, things looking good. By the time the employees figure a way out of the locked break rooms and get to a phone for some 911 action, Jimmy and Don will be at Via Deventura off Doubletree riding the confusion and delayed reactions.

They circle the block an extra time at the Via Deventura store, double-checking, but there's no sign of unmarkeds or tucked-away blue-and-whites. Nobody's expecting them.

The store turns out to be a copy of the first two. In and out. Fourteen minutes.

"Crime spree," Jimmy says, transferring the cash and coins to the first canvas bag. He imagines a slow-motion line of dominoes falling.

"Look at the box, you don't believe me," Don says, grinning. "The picture, the ceiling fan's hanging from the sky, nothing above it but blue and those puffy clouds."

Jimmy wants to hit all seven stores, one fell swoop, that's what his gut is telling him, but he's remembering how he worked it all out on paper, back at the Mesa View Inn, "applying himself" as his guidance counselor and teachers used to say, and he's sure the way the dominoes are falling, that he and Don have time for one more visit before the element of surprise completely disappears and a pattern emerges.

Four out of seven. Not bad. Jimmy can see Richard at the supper table later on in the evening, after all the police reports are filed, telling Evelyn about his day.

Jimmy directs Don down Pima toward Tempe.

TEN

Evelyn Coates watches them from behind the counter, the sudden influx of bodies a half block away as students enter or leave the southwest boundary of the campus.

She's not sure what to do with her hands. She touches her hair, the countertop, the cardboard placard advertising ASU discounts, the scanner for the register.

Finally, as if they were something she'd lured and managed to trap, Evelyn slips her hands into the pockets of the green Frontier Cleaners smock.

There's a tug high in her chest from something that's trailed her all day since breakfast.

It had been a morning like hundreds of other mornings in their marriage, Richard having shaved, showered, dressed for work, and come down to the kitchen, where he gave Evelyn a quick kiss and took the paper to the breakfast nook and worked his way through the sections, saving the crossword puzzle for last, folding the page into a neat small square, pausing to take a sip of orange juice, and then picking up a pencil.

It wasn't like Richard expected her to make breakfast. Evelyn had offered. She hadn't slept well and was up early anyway.

She had buttered and quartered the toast and was working on the eggs, two of them, sunny-side up, the way Richard always ate them, but then she had looked down into the skillet and taken the edge of the spatula and grazed each yolk, watching as their centers collapsed and yellow spooled across the whites.

It had been as if her hands belonged to someone else.

She kept waiting for Richard to say something or to hear herself offer to fry him two more, but neither happened. Richard had looked at the plate and then over at her and gone on to eat the eggs without complaint. Between bites, he had talked about an article from the paper on the city planning commission, mentioned an upcoming dinner party, and asked her if she knew a seven letter word for *passionate*.

He had been pleasant and agreeable, and the longer Evelyn sat across from him, the worse she felt. She'd gone out of her way to purposefully ruin her husband's breakfast. She'd been mean and petty, childishly vindictive. She didn't know what was wrong with her.

Evelyn takes her hands out of the pockets of the smock. The surface tension on her skin is like that of a tall glass of water filled to the brim.

She wishes she were sorry.

Evelyn remains at the counter during the long stutter of a sun-drenched afternoon. She watches the students rather than the clock. She begins to notice pieces of herself and pieces of Richard and pieces of others they knew twenty years ago, fifteen years ago, ten years ago. Outside, everything's retro, no dominant or overriding style, no distinctive generational trademark, just bits and pieces of previous decades, a fashion statement that doesn't make one, ponytails and crew cuts, chinos and bell-bottoms, button-downs and sleeveless flannels, platform heels and Birkenstocks, cowboy hats and baseball caps and bandanas, barrettes, nose pierces, peasant blouses, tattoos, sideburns, miniskirts, and Doc Martens, everything shorn of context, floating free of time and circumstance, as indiscriminate as wind-blown pollen, and for Evelyn, the sight of all those students on the street is both exhilarating and disconcerting: They've gotten away with something but don't seem to know they have.

Evelyn almost expects to see herself walk by the store. This afternoon, it seems possible. She'll look out and see herself cross the street, recognize herself at twenty, long straight hair streaked by the sun, braless under a loose-fitting white blouse tucked into tight, faded Levi's. Evelyn, done with classes, and on her way to meet her future husband at Mill Station. Evelyn, twenty, and in love.

In a blink, the image disappears. So does the street. Evelyn's looking at the slatted white backs of the blinds. There's a loud click.

Then there's a man in a baseball cap, sunglasses, and allergy mask. He's holding a gun.

The phone starts ringing.

He takes a step forward, then hesitates when she turns fully in his direction, seems to tense, acts like he might suddenly turn and leave.

The phone continues to ring.

Evelyn asks if she should answer it.

He tells her no.

Behind her from farther back in the store, someone is telling people to come on and move it.

The phone doesn't stop.

The man steps up and raps the counter with the pistol and then points it at the cash register.

"Everything," he says.

It's not the voice, no.

The rings bleed into each other, shrill and insistent.

Evelyn's hands are trembling.

"Come on," he says. "You heard me. I said everything." He looks quickly over at the telephone. It won't stop ringing.

It's not the voice, no.

It's the T-shirt.

A faded purple and orange Phoenix Suns T-shirt, a basketball sprouting flames with SCORCH 'EM printed below, the shirt wrinkled and not overly clean, the seam along the right shoulder torn and frayed. A small tuft of hair poking through. The same one she'd noticed two nights ago when she'd gone to answer the door while Richard was out back grilling salmon steaks.

Her hands are still trembling when she leans over the counter and hooks the string of the mask with her index finger and pulls it down.

"Everything?" she asks. "Even the coins, Jimmy?"

ELEVEN

There's always a pecking order, Aaron Limbe thinks. You can't get around that. Sometimes it's right up front and in your face, and at others, it's hidden, but it's there. Always.

And that's just and right and meet as far as Aaron Limbe's concerned. A pecking order serves a purpose. It clarifies things. It separates the weak from the strong, the inferior from the superior. It's necessary. God knew that. What else is Genesis if not the laying out of a grand pecking order?

God made one mistake though. If He was going to fix things after the garden and the fall, He should have made Christ a cop and sent him back to set the world straight, reestablish the law and the rightful order of things. That's what people needed, not the Mr. Softee we got stuck with. Christ just made everything worse by making excuses for everyone and calling it forgiveness. He blurred the lines of what had been there from the beginning, turning everything inside out with all that "first shall be last" lie.

Aaron Limbe wouldn't have asked for thirty pieces of silver. He'd have done it for free. Or better yet, he'd have stepped in and taken him out himself.

There's a place for everything.

People, though, have either forgotten or ignore that truth.

Aaron Limbe hasn't.

Limbe slows down when he spots two Tempe police cars set

nose to nose with their blue-and-whites flashing in front of Frontier Cleaners. He parks at the curb and studies the scene, looking at it as if through two sets of eyes, one belonging to the cop he'd been and the other to someone who's been reduced to working for a scumbag like Ray Harp.

Harp had liked the idea of having an ex-cop in his employment. Aaron Limbe had left the Phoenix Police Department barely a step ahead of the Internal Affairs Division and DA and formal charges. The evidence had been circumstantial—Limbe, after twelve years on the force, knew how to tidy up a crime scene—and Limbe figured he could have beaten the case they were trying to make if it hadn't been for the barrage of media coverage. Worried about public image, the bureaucratic boys and girls upstairs had predictably wrung their hands and then used them to cover their own asses.

Even with that, Limbe might have ridden the whole thing out.

But then, Jimmy Coates, the human monkey wrench, jammed up the works.

Ramon Delgado was a high-profile Mex lawyer who had made a name for himself defending illegal aliens and the ones who brought them in. Delgado also maintained a number of safe houses off the books, putting enough paper between himself and their operation to keep himself comfortably insulated legally. He had a white girlfriend and drove a red Mercedes. He was a hero to all the taco-benders in Phoenix and knew how to play to the liberals in the media who cast him as an updated version of Robin Hood.

Delgado and Limbe had had their share of run-ins. Leaving the courtroom after his last acquittal, Delgado had winked at Limbe.

Aaron Limbe knew this: Borders were part of the pecking order. You draw a line. This side. That side. Things are clear. Everything has its place. Once you cross a border, the balance is upset. The natural order loses its definition. Why else call them illegal aliens?

Aaron Limbe also knew this: A Mexican is nothing more than a nigger in a sombrero.

Aaron Limbe had reintroduced Ramon Delgado to his place in the pecking order.

He had staked out Delgado on his own time, waiting until the next bunch of bordergoats were set up in one of his safe houses. Limbe had then grabbed Delgado after hours in the parking lot of the Hibiscus Club and thrown him in his car.

On the front seat between them were two jumbo bags of Milky Way miniatures that Limbe had purchased earlier in the day.

Limbe drove one-handed, keeping his .38 on Delgado until Ramon had eaten the contents of both bags.

I am going to be seriously sick, Delgado had said. *Please.*

Just before he tossed Delgado's insulin works out the window, Limbe had winked at him and said, *No, you're going to be seriously dead, Ramon, and very soon.*

Limbe had then driven to the safe house. Along the way, he carefully explained to Ramon why he had to die.

Limbe had been so intent on laying things out for Delgado that he narrowly missed rear-ending a battered white pickup that had stalled beneath a traffic light.

Before he could pull around, a short dark-haired guy was at the driver's window waving some cables and asking for a jump. When the guy started to poke his head through the window, Limbe pushed him away. Delgado began yelling for help. Limbe threw the car in reverse and got out of there.

Later, he would remember his surprise that the guy had been white. The battered pickup had pure Mexican written all over it.

There had been one man watching the safe house. A skinny little guy with a Walkman, who stupidly opened the door on Limbe's first knock.

The rest of the beaners were in the back of the house, sequestered in a windowless addition. Twelve of them.

Limbe dragged Delgado into the room and had him repeat the explanation Limbe had given him earlier. If you're going to die, it's important to understand why. Every death is a lesson.

Delgado, though, was shaking and sweating and slurring his words and losing track of what he was supposed to say.

Limbe made him start over and ran him through the explanation until he got it right.

The beaners began crossing themselves.

Limbe left Delgado in the back room with them and boarded the door shut.

Then he set the place on fire.

Limbe himself called it in. He assumed—correctly as it turned out—that there'd be witnesses who could place him or his car in the Mexican quarter. He kept his story simple: He was supposed to meet a snitch in the lot of the Hibiscus Club, but the guy never showed. Limbe drove around for a while looking for him. He spotted the fire, called it in, and waited, keeping the civilians away, until the trucks and ambulance arrived.

The press and television people latched onto the fire, turning the twelve beaners into martyrs.

A few reporters also started taking a closer look at him.

He stuck to his story.

The newspaper people found a leak and got access to Limbe's personnel file and arrest records, and there were the usual claims of a long-standing pattern of intimidation and brutality and the usual clamor over departmental cover-ups and looking the other way.

The mayor felt the public pressure and eventually got involved, leaning on the police commissioner, who set in motion an IAD investigation.

Aaron Limbe was temporarily suspended.

He stuck to his story, figuring he could ride things out. The evidence did not go beyond the circumstantial. It was everybody's word against his.

Limbe was waiting for the city to tear itself apart. He had shown people where they lived. What they were. Reestablished the pecking order. There'd be no room or need for forgiveness after that.

It might have worked, too—Limbe the agent of a truth worthy of the city's namesake—if Jimmy Coates hadn't gotten picked up for grand theft auto.

At the time, Limbe had not been able to foresee, let alone prevent, what happened.

While locked up in city, Coates began reading the newspapers and recognized Limbe and Delgado. Instead of playing to the DA or IAD, Coates made noise to the chief, who then called the commissioner, and Coates went on to cut his own deal. He wanted them to lose the paperwork on the grand theft auto and explained about the jumper cable incident, italicizing the fact he could place Limbe and Delgado together the night of the murders.

The chief and commissioner saw the opportunity to quickly clean house and avoid the fallout from the publicity of a trial. Limbe was called in and the situation laid out. The chief and commissioner had already signed his resignation papers. He was handed a pen.

After Limbe left the force, nobody else, not even the private security companies, would touch him.

That's what he'd become. Untouchable.

For a month, he'd averaged eight pieces of hate mail a day. He'd hoped for more.

It had taken a long time for Limbe to find out the name of the guy with the jumper cables and white pickup. The brass had put a tight lid on the paperwork for the case. Limbe was patient. He waited and quietly asked around, and he eventually hooked up with a few right-thinking white guys on the force who were willing to do a favor for someone who'd once been one of their own.

As soon as he got the name, Limbe set out to kill Coates, only to discover Coates was doing time in Perryville Correctional after having been popped with a tractor-trailer load of black-market saguaros.

So Aaron Limbe had to wait.

He was untouchable. While he waited, he began to understand exactly what that meant.

He snaps to. He's not sure how long he's been parked at the curb watching the lights on the blue-and-white strobing the front windows of the dry-cleaning shop. He feels the beginnings of a headache blooming at the base of his skull. He climbs out of his car carrying two of Ray Harp's metallic blue three-piece suits and crosses the street. He recognizes one of the Tempe cops, a guy named Henderson, and strolls into the middle of the crime scene.

Henderson tips back his cap and scratches his forehead. "Come on, Aaron, you know the drill."

"I'm just curious is all," Limbe says. "What you got, a straight armed? I don't see any blood." A few feet away a woman with dark blond hair is giving a statement to a fresh-deck rookie.

"You shouldn't be here," Henderson says, still going at his forehead.

"I know." Limbe smiles. He watches the woman, listens to the spin she puts on her words. He unwraps a breath mint, slips it on his tongue.

"You can bring those back tomorrow," Henderson says, pointing at the suits.

"Who's the Gash?" Limbe asks, nodding in the blond's direction.

Henderson shakes his head and sighs. "The owner's wife. She was working the register."

"She's nervous," Limbe says.

"Of course, she's nervous," Henderson says. "She just got held up."

The rookie cop takes everything the woman says down. He's polite and attentive. Limbe smiles. She's nervous all right. But not because someone stuck a gun in her face. Aaron Limbe's been around enough crime scenes to read a witness.

"What did you say her name was?" he asks.

"Coates. Evelyn Coates," Henderson says.

Limbe takes in the last name and smiles and listens to the rookie read back her description of the perp. She nods one too many times.

Limbe considers telling Henderson that his primary witness is lying through her teeth.

He doesn't though.

Instead, he files it away.

TWELVE

Jimmy wishes he'd had a say in where he was to meet Evelyn. He's got this thing about Scottsdale. The place gets on his nerves. It's one of those peculiar American cities, like Key West, that have mortgaged their history with charm. The place started out in the late 1800s as nothing more than a bunch of tents and adobe houses that catered to lung cases from back East, but by the 1930s, Scottsdale was promising more than cures, branching out into recreation and elegance, the tents giving way to high-profile hotels and rustic resorts promising desert vistas; and with more big bucks pouring in from back East, Scottsdale began billing itself as the "West's Most Western Town," continually feeding the myth and enlarging its allure, reinventing itself to the tune of 183,000 square miles, the place now a trendy hybrid of the biggest lies from the Old and New West, the tourists and locals, as if by unspoken agreement, conspiring to hold each other hostage to its fabled charm. Everything in Scottsdale had the feel of something italicized, the place doubling as noun and its own adjective.

When Jimmy gets to the country club, he's relieved to see Evelyn's reserved a table in the smoking section. His server's name is Peter, the guy coming down hard on the first syllable and letting up on the gas for the second. Jimmy tells Pete he wants a cold one and then torches a Marlboro.

The table's next to a window. Below Jimmy is a bunch of flowerbeds, then two small ponds ringed by palms and boxwoods, and in the distance, a cluster of golfers teeing up.

Eighteen hours since the Tempe job and he hasn't been arrested yet.

None of it makes any sense.

Even though Evelyn had made him at the scene, she had handed over the money in the register and the safe, but then told him if he tried to leave town, she'd call the police and turn him in.

Jimmy sips at his beer. Evelyn shows up a half hour late.

He watches her cross the room, pausing to say hello to some of the moms, waving and smiling at a couple of tables of suits, the ghost of her years as a flight attendant in the way she carries herself. Her hair's just brushing her shoulders. It's the color of a slice of wheat bread. She's wearing a red sundress covered in clusters of tiny yellow flowers. Jimmy reflexively checks out the cleavage, and he's thrown off a little because the breasts aren't as big as he remembers. Not that Evelyn's lacking in the chest department—a view's a view—but Jimmy can't help feeling like he did when, as a kid, he first saw Mount Rushmore, the real thing just not matching up with the idea he'd been carrying around in his head.

Evelyn sits down across from him and pushes her sunglasses high on her forehead. Pete, the server, nods, and without her having to order, delivers a large martini.

Jimmy lights a cigarette. Evelyn waits, head tilted, until he offers her one.

"I didn't know you smoked," he says, sliding the pack over.

"Family secret," she says and waits again until Jimmy lights it for her.

"I can't imagine Richard there, him lighting one up for you."

"Richard doesn't know everything about me," Evelyn says, "and neither do you."

"Hey, you're a complicated person," Jimmy says. "We've established that."

"You don't like me very much, do you, Jimmy?"

Jimmy takes a sip of beer.

"You think you have me all figured out. I'm the second half of a boxed set in your eyes." Evelyn raises her hand, and Pete's right there with another martini.

"What do you want me to say? You married the guy, stayed with him, what, going on eighteen years? Your choice. I didn't have one. That's the thing about brothers. You're stuck with what you get."

Evelyn studies him over the rim of her drink. There's a light flush building at the base of her throat and slowly spreading upward. She takes another of Jimmy's cigarettes and lights it herself this time.

"Anyway," Jimmy says, "what does how I see you have anything to do with why we're here?"

"It does, Jimmy. It has a lot to do with it."

Jimmy leans back in his chair and looks at the ceiling. "Am I missing something here?"

"It wouldn't be the first time, that's for sure." Evelyn's pointing at him with the cigarette when he lowers his head.

"Okay. Tell me this. How'd you make me for the robbery?"

She explains about the T-shirt, the split seam, and the tuft of shoulder hair.

Jimmy starts laughing, despite himself. "I got to give it to you, Evelyn. That was good, you noticing that. You were supposed to be looking at the gun."

"Afraid for my life," Evelyn says.

"That's the general idea, yes."

Pete comes up for their lunch order, Evelyn going with a Greek salad and another martini, Jimmy a burger, heavy on the mustard and mayo, some house fries, and another cold one.

After ordering, there's an awkward silence, Jimmy figuring since he's about to eat lunch at the Scottsdale Country Club that Evelyn hasn't told Richard what she knows about the robberies, but Jimmy not sure how to maneuver to keep it that way. The Evelyn sitting across from him is not the one he's used to dealing with.

She's turned quarter-profile from him when she suddenly asks, "Would you give me the money back if I asked for it?"

"Fact of the matter, I'd rather keep it. But I guess if you were going to turn me over to the cops if I didn't, then, yeah, I guess I'd give you back my share."

"Your share? Not the whole thing?"

"You made me, Evelyn, not my partner. He did what he was supposed to, so I gave him his share."

"What would you do if I said you had to give him up to keep from going to jail?"

"Like I said, Evelyn, this is between me and you, not him."

"Would he do the same for you?"

"I don't know," Jimmy says. "Probably not. For one, he's got a family. Another thing is he's afraid of prison." Jimmy pauses to light a cigarette. "So you want the money back, that's it?"

She shakes her head no. "I don't care about the money."

"Then what was the point, all the questions?"

"I'm trying to get a better sense of who you are, Jimmy."

Jimmy slowly shakes his head from side to side. "Hey, unlike you, Evelyn, I'm not very complicated. I'm just a regular guy."

"No," Evelyn says, flushing. "What you are is full of shit. You're patronizing me, Jimmy."

Pete brings up a little two-tiered tray with lunch.

Evelyn's ordered another martini before he's done setting out the food. Pete glances over at Jimmy. "You the designated?"

Jimmy tells Pete he's the designated waiter and not to worry about it. Evelyn's turned back to the window again, and the noon light's not going easy on her. She looks like she hasn't slept in a while. She's lost the poise and the carefully constructed beauty Jimmy's always associated with her. The seams are showing today.

After Pete leaves, Evelyn pushes her salad aside and asks, "Why'd you rob Frontier Cleaners in the first place? Why not something else?"

Jimmy ticks the side of his beer glass. "Richard took something that belonged to me. I wanted him to know what it felt like."

"You mean your grandfather's place?" Evelyn pauses, furrowing her brow. "According to Richard, he saved it."

"Well 'according to Richard' is not the same as 'according to Jimmy.' We're talking different species of the truth here. My grandfather intended for that land to be mine. My dad knew that. Richard knew that, too."

"He took your dad's death hard," Evelyn says. "It changed him in ways I'm not sure he's even aware of."

Jimmy shakes his head. "No way it changed him. It just made him more of what he already was."

"That's harsh, Jimmy. Unfair, too."

Jimmy slowly lets out his breath. "Look, Evelyn, to get back to the point here, I don't want to end up in prison again."

She takes a large swallow of her drink. "I don't blame you."

"And I don't want to die either," Jimmy says, "which is what Ray Harp's got lined up for me unless I get him his cash."

"I told you already." Evelyn waves her fingers. "You can have it."

"I'm glad to hear that," Jimmy says. "What you haven't told me is what you want in return."

There's no focus to Evelyn's smile. It's floating, separate from her features like the lipstick smudges on the rim of her glass.

The smile goes on too long. The same deal with the eyes, the blue unwavering gaze she's training on him.

"What I want," she says, "is to commit a crime."

"Get real," Jimmy says, looking around.

"I am," she says. "That's what I want. A crime. I want to commit a crime, and I want to get away with it, and I want you to help me do it."

"Come on," Jimmy says. "You? That doesn't make any sense."

Evelyn aims the smile at him again.

THIRTEEN

O*nly one thing,* Jimmy had told her. *I set something up, no guns. No way, guns.*

Evelyn had gone along with that, but still wanted to learn to shoot.

Which is why she's riding in Jimmy's pickup this afternoon. The windows are open, filling the cab with a hot rush of air. Evelyn's got her feet propped against the dash. She's humming a tune the radio might have played if it worked.

Jimmy's routing them through a series of back roads toward Dobbins. They pass a stretch of homes that tried out for the middle class but got cut from the team, and then after the land opens a little, they pass small horse farms and wide, flat soybean and cotton fields. Every now and then, he'll catch a thin glint of light from the surface of the city's canal system. When the wind shifts, there's the smell of the stockyards to the west, a rich heavy smell like stale chocolate floating in warm spoiled milk.

Ahead, South Mountain National Park enfolds the southern boundary of Phoenix. From this distance, the mountains resemble an immense open accordion lying on its back.

"Loosen up, Jimmy. You're acting like a little boy who's been forced to invite a girl to his birthday party."

Jimmy keeps his eyes on the road. "This Bonnie and Clyde thing you cooked up, you sure you want to go through with it?"

"We made an agreement, Jimmy. Nothing's changed."

Jimmy starts tapping the top of the steering wheel. "Why are you doing this? I still don't get it."

Evelyn reaches back and lifts her hair from the back of her neck, holding it up one-handed. "Don't worry about my reasons. Just hold up your end." She waits a moment, then looks over at Jimmy and says, "Speaking of which."

"I'm setting something up, okay? I'll fill you in, all the details, when you're done shooting."

"Sounds good." Evelyn lets her hair fall back down over her shoulders.

Jimmy turns right on Dobbins, heading west. The farmhouse is a stucco rectangle setting atop a flattened crest, a long gravel drive curving along its eastern boundary.

He stops in front of a shiny new aluminum gate that Richard had put up. He gets out and picks the lock, then hops back into the truck, moving up the drive, the gravel jumping under the tires and popcorning the truck's undercarriage.

"When I was a kid," Jimmy says, pointing out the window, "my grandfather told me there was buried treasure on the place. Supposed to belong to a gang of outlaws who came to a bad end. Untold wealth, that's what he said. The son of a bitch even went so far, drew out a map on some ratty paper, and then passed it off to me as something his grandfather had taken from a dead man's pockets. Hell, I was eight years old. I believed him. Every chance I got, I was out here with a shovel. Gramps, there, sitting on the back porch in a lawn chair, big tumblerful of bourbon, egging me on."

"What about Richard?" Evelyn asks. "Did he help you look?"

"Nah," Jimmy says. "Richard, he had a paper route. Two of them actually. Even then he was branching out."

Jimmy parks the truck on the gravel apron next to the house and gets out. The whole place has gone feral. He can barely match memory to fact.

The dark brown stucco walls of the house have been weather-worn to a dirty tan. The roof on the back porch has partially collapsed. There's a papery gray hornet's nest, squat and bulbous as a basketball, hanging from the eaves above the kitchen window. The front lawn, or what once passed for it, is four acres of tangle and choke.

Until Richard put up the gate, for over two decades the locals had been using the back seventeen acres as a dumping ground. Scattered among the evenly spaced rows of the orchard Jimmy remembers—now nothing more than a bunch of brittle sticks holding sickly golf-ball-sized oranges and lemons—are televisions and refrigerators and stoves and sofas and bedsprings and mattresses, piles of bald tires, an installment plan graveyard, even a rust-eaten carcass of an old Chevy Nova, sunk onto its shocks, its windows and engine missing.

It's not the memories or the present state of things that matters though. What matters is the dirt under his feet and who holds the deed to it. Twenty undeveloped acres in a city ringed by mountains and very little space to grow. What matters is the raw potential, the cash cow that his brother had taken from him.

Jimmy watches Evelyn climb out of the truck.

He then walks into the ghost of the orchard and sets up targets—old paint cans, glass bottles, beer cans—on the spindly limbs and outcroppings of rocks. He walks back to the truck and takes out a canvas bag holding a Colt Diamondback .38 and enough ammunition to wipe out Utah. He loads the Diamondback and hands it to Evelyn.

"Pull the trigger," he says, "and you're in business."

Jimmy drags the cooler from the bed of the truck and cracks a beer. Evelyn's positioned herself about ten yards from the targets. Jimmy sits down on the lid of the cooler. He's got an unencumbered view of the skyline of Phoenix, no thermal inversions, the day clear enough that he can see past Squaw Peak to the mountains on the city's far northern rim. In the middle distance is Sky Harbor International, and he watches three jets circle and make their approach, wings blinking in the sun as they bank.

Evelyn's watched too much television. She's got herself set up in an elaborate shooter's stance that might make for high drama on a cop show but won't do her any good out here. She misses everything she fires at and walks over to the cooler.

She's wearing a pair of faded denim shorts, a crisp white T-shirt, and a pair of espadrilles. No makeup or sunglasses. She's pale-skinned, the shade you find on the inside of an orange peel.

Jimmy gives her a beer and shows her how to reload the Colt. He's not in the mood to do much more than that right now. She takes a box of bullets and goes back to her original position and starts blasting away.

This whole crime thing, Jimmy has no intention of disappointing Evelyn and landing himself back in prison, not now when he can use the green from his share of the dry-cleaning holdups to get himself clear with Ray Harp.

Jimmy also has no intention of ending up in prison again from committing a crime with an amateur for a partner.

He's set something up that's safe and sweet.

Yesterday, Pete Samoa had intro'ed Jimmy to a guy named Vic Stamp, who owns a large volume-discount shoe store. Vic has a little problem with some of his stock, in particular, a line of athletic shoes he can't move, the shoes neon green on purple with thick yellow soles and flashing red lights embedded on the sides of the heels. That they're ugly is bad enough, but the death kiss on sales is the dye they used on them, which has the unfortunate tendency to run every time the shoes get wet.

The manufacturer, after stalling on returns, has gone Chapter Eleven, so Vic Stamp's stuck with five hundred pairs of Force One footwear. He needs someone to come in and rip off the overstock so he can collect on the insurance.

The job's a straight grand, plus whatever Jimmy can lay off the shoes for. Pete Samoa's offered to pick up the lot for seventy-five cents a pair, which Pete will then turn around and fence through a deal he's cut with one of the government agents on the reservations.

Everybody's happy. Evelyn gets her crime. Vic collects on the insurance. Pete turns a tidy profit. Jimmy pockets his share of the thousand and can pay the balance on what he owes Ray Harp.

And until the first rainstorm, five hundred Native American kids will have some snazzy new sneakers.

Evelyn will never have to know about the insurance angle. Jimmy can pass the job off as a straight burglary, giving it a little glamour and danger to sweeten it up for her. Vic Stamp wants them to hit the store tomorrow night when they're doing after-hours inventory. He's arranged it so the manager will go on break around ten and forget to set the alarm. Jimmy and Evelyn will have a little less than thirty minutes to get in and out.

Jimmy lifts his head at the sound of glass breaking. Evelyn's finally zapped a target. She walks over and Jimmy gives her a beer, takes another for himself. Evelyn's face is flushed from the heat, and there's a dark wedge of sweat running from the neckline of her T-shirt to the middle of her chest.

"Shooting's harder than I thought it would be," she says, tilting back the can.

"That's your problem," Jimmy says. "Thinking about it. You shouldn't do that. You need to think with your body."

"How are you supposed to do that?"

"You jumped rope when you were a girl, right? You start thinking about jumping rope, you can't do it. You'll trip yourself up. Same thing with shooting a gun."

Evelyn finishes the beer and drops the can on the ground. "Show me," she says.

Jimmy reloads the Diamondback and walks over to where Evelyn had stood earlier. He points out three bottles he'd set among the limbs of a dying lemon tree and two cans resting on top of a ledge of rock. He takes a deep breath and slowly lets it out, then raises his arm and gets off five quick shots, hitting everything but one of the cans.

"I thought you didn't like guns," Evelyn says.

"I don't. But that doesn't mean I don't know how to use them." He hands Evelyn the Colt. She steps up and points out two cans.

"Those," she says.

"TV time," Jimmy says, shaking his head. He walks over and

puts his hand on the small of Evelyn's back and presses so that she drops the semicrouch action and stands straighter.

"You don't need both arms either," he says, reaching over and disengaging her left hand from where she's locked it to her right wrist. "The Diamondback's not that heavy."

He tells her to stand there for a minute and breathe. Empty her mind of everything, then simply raise her arm and fire.

She misses both cans. But not by as much as earlier.

"This time, the trigger," Jimmy says, stepping closer. "You're pulling the trigger and throwing off your aim. Squeeze it instead."

Jimmy stands just behind Evelyn's right shoulder. He reaches down and lays his arm over hers, encircling her wrist with his fingers, and moves her arm so that the gun is pointing straight down. He keeps his arm where it is.

"Do like I told you," he says. "Breathe."

Evelyn has her hair pulled back in a careless ponytail, and there are two small moles side by side where her hairline meets her neck. Her skin's flushed from the heat and lacquered with a thin sheen of sweat. He smells traces of sunscreen and shampoo. He leans closer and whispers into the seashell whorl of her ear, "Don't think. Move when I do. Then squeeze."

He lifts her arm in one fluid movement and stops. She fires. The can somersaults off the ledge.

"The other one now," he says, turning her slightly. She's not wearing a bra. Her breast shifts and bunches against the underside of his arm.

She squeezes. The second can jumps and disappears into a thicket of mesquite.

He's about to let go of her arm when she turns her head.

She hesitates. Then he does.

He's thinking she's going to step to the side and away.

She doesn't.

He has no idea how long the kiss lasts.

Neither of them says anything when they break apart. Jimmy can see her nipples through the T-shirt. A muscle in his stomach jumps.

"I'll decide if that happened or not," Evelyn says.

Jimmy looks at her, shakes his head, and then walks back over to the cooler.

A few seconds later, there's a pistol shot. Jimmy ducks.

The hornet's nest under the eaves of the house explodes.

Fifteen yards away, Evelyn lowers her arm and slowly lets out her breath.

FOURTEEN

Aaron Limbe hangs back, keeping at least six cars between him and the truck. He's working his own clock tonight, not Ray Harp's, and holding the tail's about as difficult as striking a match. The truck's a boxy rental, a caution-light yellow, with an enclosed bed. Coates is sticking to the center lane, going north on route 17.

Limbe had trusted to instinct and staked out the Mesa View Inn, and Coates and his sister-in-law had not disappointed him. She had pulled up in the yellow rental a little after 9:00 P.M. and headed straight for room 110. They left ten minutes later.

Tonight, Limbe misses his uniform, the night-blue fit, its sharp, precise creases, the weight of the badge on its pocket. Buttoning the shirt had been as familiar as writing his signature. He misses the way the uniform placed him and established boundaries.

At times like this, when thinking of his fall from the police department or of being reduced to working for a lowlife like Ray Harp, it becomes a test of Limbe's will not to simply go on and kill Coates outright.

But he must stay strong, he tells himself, and inhabit what he knows.

Jimmy Coates is the last tie to Limbe's old life. His death cannot be insignificant.

Aaron Limbe must get it right.

Jimmy Coates must fully learn the nature and breadth of consequence.

Aaron Limbe unwraps a breath mint and slips it onto his tongue.

Besides, he thinks, the sister-in-law is a wrinkle he hadn't expected.

The rental truck's turn signal comes to life, and Limbe follows it off the Camelback Road exit, Coates heading west now, toward Glendale.

The sky's lower than the mountains tonight, thick and churning with clouds strong-armed by constant winds and skeined by lightning. Everything's in motion.

Coates slows as he passes Shoe City. The lights in the store are on, but no cars are in the lot. There's a portable billboard out front advertising an Inventory Reduction Sale starting tomorrow and a large revolving shoe sprouting from the store's roof.

Coates takes the next side street off Camelback and pulls in behind the store.

Aaron Limbe goes on for a block and circles back. He parks away from the halogen light on the corner under a line of date palms and watches Coates back the truck up to the loading bay. Above Limbe, the palm fronds snap and rattle in the wind.

Jimmy Coates stands outside the truck for a moment, looking around, and then climbs up on the loading bay. Evelyn Coates gets out and opens the rear door of the truck.

Aaron Limbe grips the steering wheel. He can feel the storm coming in, the sudden drop in barometric pressure, the wind shifting from a hiss to a roar, grit and sand pinging against his car, the palms' clatter now sounding like a pencil thrust between the blades of a fan.

The headaches again.

Not now, he tells himself.

He wills back the sky.

But it's as if the wind has found its way into the veins running beneath both temples. Limbe looks down at his hands white-knuckling the steering wheel and then slowly lifts his left and cups the crown of his head.

If he's not careful, the headaches take him away from himself.

Through a tight squint, Limbe watches Jimmy Coates and his sister-in-law scramble, moving armloads of boxes from the rear of the store and dumping them in the truck. As they cross the loading bay, the wind rips the top off most of the boxes, scattering them across the lot and pinning them to the wire fence bordering the street.

Limbe takes his camera and gets out of the car. His hands are shaking so badly that for a moment he's not even sure he can get the lens cap off, let alone work the camera. His fingers are thick and awkward, refusing to cooperate with him or each other. The roar inside his head is indistinguishable from the wind and erases every other sound.

Limbe leans over the hood of the car. He hears Jimmy Coates yell something to his sister-in-law, but Aaron can't make out what. The wind is still roaring around him. He straightens, lifting the camera, and gets off three shots before the clouds break open.

It's a punishing rain, hard and intense and unyielding, sweeping from the east in great gusting sheets. Limbe is instantly soaked to his skin.

The rain doesn't let up. Within minutes the gutters are overflowing, water rushing everywhere. It pulls one of the car's hubcaps free. The wipers can't clear the weight of the rain and freeze up in the middle of the windshield. The air turns thick and close, and it feels like someone's pressing a damp washcloth over his face.

Limbe rests his forehead on the steering wheel and lets the storm pass through him.

He has no idea how long it takes for the sky to clear. When he lifts his head, the doors to the loading bay are closed and the yellow rental is gone. The lot behind the store is completely flooded, the water dark and muddy, still now that the wind has disappeared, and dotted with palm fronds and sheets of newspaper and styrofoam cups and clusters of shoeboxes floating like tiny coffins torn from the earth.

FIFTEEN

Jimmy snaps out a black plastic bag, then starts stripping the bed at the Mesa View Inn. The sheets are stained purple and green.

When he gets to the pillowcase, he smiles.

He's figured out a way to pay his brother back.

After last night, he's got all the ammo he needs.

Neither Evelyn or he had noticed the stains until they were back in the truck headed toward Phoenix and Pete Samoa's Pawn Emporium. The rain had drenched them as well as the merchandise, whose dyes, as Vic Stamp had lamented, leached and bled at the first sign of moisture. Jimmy's and Evelyn's hands and arms as far as their elbows were tattooed in purple and green.

Pete winked and slipped Jimmy the envelope Vic had left for him holding the grand but then went over the edge when he opened the doors of the rental and saw the condition of the shoes. After a few minutes of yelling and cursing, Pete slipped directly into his renegotiation mode, refusing to stand by his original offer of seventy-five cents a pair, claiming he couldn't do better than a quarter per for damaged goods, Jimmy and Evelyn ganging up on him, refusing to help him unload the truck unless he went fifty. Pete bitched and moaned some more, and they settled on forty-five cents per pair.

Jimmy and Evelyn returned the rental and picked up Evelyn's car, and she took him back to the Mesa View, Evelyn still pumped up from the job, wanting to replay the details and side-order how she'd felt throughout, Evelyn doing a pretty good imitation of a crank monologue, and Jimmy let her run, interrupting only when necessary to point out a couple of things that would have given the Phoenix police an invitation to ruin the party, like Evelyn's tendency to run yellow lights and improvise on the speed limit.

It was going on midnight when they got back to his room. Evelyn popped the trunk on the Mustang and produced a fifth of Wild Turkey she'd lifted from Richard's wet bar. She wanted a celebratory drink to close their deal and to clean up some before she went home. Jimmy unlocked the door to the room and hunted down some glasses and ice.

They poured a couple. Evelyn bracketed each with corny movie-line toasts, acting as if they'd pulled off the heist of the century instead of lifting a pile of defective athletic shoes. He let her count out the the split from Pete Samoa, Evelyn squaring the bills in neat little piles in front of her and touching them whenever she lifted her drink.

Jimmy hadn't been thinking of the kiss. He'd been thinking instead of the envelope in his back pocket holding the grand, which, in addition to his share from the dry-cleaning holdups, would finally clear the books with Ray Harp and ransom himself from another session in the desert with the dog collar or something worse. Jimmy had simply been unwinding behind the whiskey, glad that the job earlier in the evening had gone okay and that he was off the hook with Evelyn now and on the verge of getting his old life back.

No way had he been thinking about the kiss. The room itself conspired against it, the ambience of the Mesa View's decor not exactly bringing to mind a love nest.

Jimmy still can't say for sure what the trigger was for them ending up in bed, but they had, and he can remember the surprise of fingers and tongues all right, of unsnapping Evelyn's bra and leaving green fingerprints on her breasts, of flesh giving way to flesh and the wind of breath in his ear, of Evelyn wet and locking her legs around his waist, meeting each of his thrusts with one of her own, Evelyn's voice mixed in there, too, low and insistent, urging him on, the muscles in her legs beginning to tighten and shudder, Evelyn pushing harder against him, wet and tight and soaking his crotch, then her voice breaking, Evelyn throwing back her head and coming, her legs squeezing him and her mouth open, the surprising, oddly intimate glimpse of her back molars and pink tunnel of throat unexpectedly jacking him to his own orgasm.

Evelyn had immediately dropped off to sleep. Jimmy, used to being the recipient of the universal postcoital complaint, remained wide awake. After fifteen minutes of alternately staring at the ceiling and at Evelyn splayed on the bed beside him, he got up and made a drink.

He ended up making a couple of more before he picked up Evelyn's panties and slipped them inside his pillowcase and went to take a shower.

He'd managed to scrub off most of the green and purple patchwork of stains when Evelyn stepped in and joined him, Jimmy feeling put on the spot, telling her he might need a little more turnaround time if she was thinking repeat performances, Evelyn looking him right in the eye and smiling as she began to soap up her hands.

Five minutes later, still wet from the shower, they were back in bed.

Evelyn left for home a little before 3:00 A.M.

Jimmy, whistling, keeps snapping out plastic bags and filling them with laundry. It's an old tune, one that anyone would recognize.

SIXTEEN

Richard keeps leaning across the table and waving the tickets in her face.

"You forgot?" he asks. "I mean, how is that possible? I've been talking about it for over a month. You even marked it on the calendar."

"Okay," Evelyn says, picking up her coffee cup. "I didn't forget. I just can't go right now."

Richard looks out the bay window of the breakfast nook and asks why.

"Carol's going through a rough time," Evelyn says. "She needs me. I'm her friend."

"She's got plenty of other friends," Richard says, "if she needs someone to hold her hand. Besides, you know what I think about you hanging out with her in the first place. Carol's never been very stable."

Yes, Evelyn knows what Richard thinks about Carol Findley. She owns and runs a small gallery in Scottsdale. Richard usually refers to her as "one of those art types," a convenient shorthand dismissal on his part from ever having to get to know her. Which is why Evelyn used her as a cover, the odds next to none that Richard would ever call Carol and check up on any of the details Evelyn's been feeding him lately.

"The tickets are already paid for," Richard says, "and we have reservations at the Marriott on Peachtree near the convention center. I can't cancel now."

"You can still go," Evelyn says.

Richard doesn't say anything. He looks like he's been slapped. He glances at the clock and then gets up and walks over to the refrigerator to make a sandwich. He'd come home during his lunch hour to oversee packing for the trip. Evelyn got back sometime after 3:30 last night and had just been getting out of bed.

"It won't be all business, you know." He's at the counter, his back to her. "We can take some time for ourselves, too."

Evelyn knows what that means. It's Richard's elliptical way of resurrecting the issue of starting a family. When she first quit the airlines he had pushed hard on their having a child; and when Evelyn balked, told him she wasn't sure if she wanted one, Richard had backed off some, stoically accepting her wishes but not giving up on the idea of a child, confident that in the end Evelyn would come around, Richard nothing if not patient; but after his father died, Richard had started pushing hard again, and things between them were always tense, their lives together like the slow grinding of teeth or the steady leak of a faucet; and for Richard, Atlanta must have seemed like the perfect opportunity, a little time together, Evelyn surely coming to her senses and seeing he'd been right all along.

"I'd like you there with me." His voice quiet and even.

"I'm sorry," Evelyn says.

"That's it? You're sorry? What does that mean exactly?" Richard's turned partway around, holding a knife in one hand, a jar of mayonnaise in the other.

"I don't want to go to Atlanta right now, that's all."

Richard turns back to the counter and the sandwich. He has all the ingredients laid out with the efficiency and precision of an assembly line, and after he finishes one he picks up a plate and starts over. He then peels and cores a bright green Granny Smith, cutting the apple neatly in two and setting half on each plate. He pours two glasses of ice water. He brings everything over to the table and takes off his jacket. Evelyn notices small flecks of gray in his hair. The skin around his eyes is still smooth and unlined. Her husband has always worn his age well.

He's about to take the first bite of his sandwich when he notices the blinking red light of the answering machine on the other side of the kitchen. He asks Evelyn if she checked the messages. She shakes her head no. He frowns and gets up. One's from an electrician, then a plumber, and finally a subcontractor. Richard copies down a series of numbers in a small notebook he's taken from his shirt pocket.

"What was that about?" Evelyn, suddenly ravenous, goes on to finish half her sandwich in three bites.

"Some estimates for work on the farmhouse. The place is a mess. I'd like to get a couple crews out there soon."

"Have you told your brother what you're planning to do?"

Richard shakes his head and picks up his sandwich. "The place is legally mine, Evelyn. What I decide to do with it doesn't concern him."

"Doesn't it bother you?" Evelyn begins.

"No," Richard says, momentarily lowering his sandwich.

Evelyn looks away. In the backyard, three Inca doves tumble through the air as if pulled on strings.

She half listens to Richard talk about his plans for renovating the farmhouse, for clearing and landscaping the surrounding property, turning the place into a weekend getaway for them, Evelyn not wanting to meet her husband's eyes, saddened and afraid of what she sees there, of what they held and did not hold ever since his father died, Richard burying him as methodically and efficiently as he made the sandwiches earlier, then dutifully stepping in and straightening out the tangle his father left his estate in, Richard keeping his grief to himself or holding it at arm's length as he went about the business of running his business and making plans, Evelyn a reluctant witness to it all, feeling as if her father-in-law's corpse had moved into every room of the house and her husband started and ended each day by once again burying him.

Below the bay window is a thick cluster of hibiscus swollen with large orange-salmon blooms and the small, buzzing orbits of bees. The entire backyard is coated in the flat light of the noon sun.

Richard has set the airline tickets on the table between them.

Evelyn thinks of standing on the loading bay of the shoe store off Camelback Road last night, her arms full of stolen goods, the lash of the wind and rain on her face, of something large and unwieldy tearing loose inside her that this kitchen, the noon light, and Atlanta cannot touch.

She committed a crime.

And she liked it.

Yes, she did.

A crime for its own sake, no overriding reason behind it, a wrongful act not tainted by motive, Evelyn breaking the law simply because there was a law that could be broken. She stepped across a line that everything in her upbringing and personality had told her she couldn't and shouldn't do. She'd wanted to inhabit the absolute clarity of transgression just once and get away with it.

And she had.

Of what happened later at the Mesa View Inn, that she doesn't want to think about. At least not right now.

"Evelyn," Richard says softly, pausing, Evelyn expecting him to go on, but that's it, her name, and then Richard takes a bite of his sandwich.

She can't picture it, or rather she can picture it all too easily, three days in Atlanta at the American Dry Cleaners Association's annual convention; three days of brochures and displays of the latest equipment; of demonstrations for improved solvents; of Internet workshops for small businesses; of name tags and handshakes and corny, slightly off-color jokes and watered-down drinks and hotel food; of Evelyn standing by Richard's side and smiling, smiling, smiling; and Evelyn suddenly wants to cry, because eighteen-plus years of marriage have turned into those two tickets to Atlanta, have become something she can't picture anymore or can picture all too easily.

She reaches across the table and takes Richard's hand.

"We could cash the tickets in," she says. "Forget Atlanta altogether. Take some time off like you said, just you and me. We'll rent a car and drive, not worry about where."

For a moment, she sees something move across his features.

Yes, she thinks.

But then Richard squeezes her hand and says, "I can't no-show on this one, Evelyn. Jack Thomas is retiring, stepping down as president of the association. I'm supposed to give the keynote address at the dinner honoring him."

"Can't someone else do it?"

"Bad form. Especially in light of the talk that I'm in the running to be named as his successor." Richard frowns and takes a sip of ice water. "We've been over this before. None of it should be news to you, Evelyn."

"I suppose not," she says.

SEVENTEEN

Jimmy's not sure if you're supposed to sort on the basis of color or fabric or both, figures in the larger scheme of things the distinction doesn't matter—clean's clean—and lifts the lids on four consecutive top-loaders and crams them with the sum total of his wardrobe, dumps in some detergent, and goes with the Big H times three—Hot, High, Heavy—slotting in the coins, and then cutting across the room to a row of orange plastic chairs lining the front windows of the Laundromat and dropping into one, the afternoon sun warming the glass and the back of his neck.

The Laundromat's two long blocks from his room at the Mesa View Inn, its interior bathed in the nervous, overly bright light from banks of naked fluorescents set in the ceiling, the walls a faded two-tone, industrial green against pink, the linoleum floor checkerboarded with missing tiles and sticky from spilled soft drinks and detergent, everything overlaid with the clank and hiss and hum of the washers and dryers and the resolute smell of bleach.

Besides Jimmy, there are four women in the mat. Once the clothes are going, Jimmy picks up the manila envelope lying on the table next to the wrinkled pile of plastic bags he'd carted his laundry in, and walks out the door.

On the corner, a block and a half to the west, is a squat blue mailbox. He still has time to make the afternoon pickup.

He switches the manila envelope to his right hand and starts walking toward the corner.

He should be feeling better than he is. He's found a perfect payback for his brother maneuvering him out of his inheritance.

Hell, if Jimmy wants to push it, a perfect payback for his brother's attitude all the way through childhood—Richard, the Alex Trebek of siblings, the same swarmy Mr. Nice Guy arrogance and sugar-coated contempt masquerading as humility, the guy who smugly controlled the board and knew both the questions and answers.

Before last night, Evelyn was the one pulling all the strings. She could turn him in to the police at any time for the robberies at Frontier Cleaners.

But Evelyn had wanted a crime. One of her own. Jimmy delivered it up. The strings changed hands. Evelyn had rented the truck in her name. And when she crossed the loading bay with the first armload of shoeboxes, she moved from innocent bystander to accomplice to felon.

Evelyn got the thrills she wanted plus a little of the unbargained for. She couldn't finger Jimmy for the dry-cleaning robberies without him in turn implicating her in the Vic Stamp Shoe City job. A Scottsdale matron hitting a discount shoe mart. After teaming up with her brother-in-law, who'd hit four out of seven of his brother's dry-cleaning stores in one afternoon. The press and Evelyn and Richard's neighbors would love it. It was almost worth a return trip to Perryville Correctional.

Almost.

The sex had been an unexpected perk, one that again Jimmy had not seen clearly at the time because he was having too much fun engaging in it.

His brother was about to take the long fall.

There was no need to bring the neighbors or press or anybody else into it. A guy like Richard, his temperament, just knowing how close his personal life and professional reputation had been to public scandal, that was torment enough. The potential for disgrace would stay with him, move right into his life, and Richard, being Richard, would feed it, keep it alive.

All Jimmy has to do is drop Evelyn's panties in the mail.

He's got the manila envelope addressed to Richard, the correct postage tucked in the upper right-hand corner, no return address, and no accompanying note, just a pack of matches from the Mesa View Inn and Evelyn's silky blue panties, on whose crotch he'd taken a pen and inked the date she'd stayed with him at the Mesa View.

Jimmy figures he'll let Richard puzzle over them for a day before he picks up the phone and enlightens him as to their ownership.

And while he's at it, fill Richard in on who robbed the four Frontier Cleaners stores. As well as who let Jimmy walk on the last one. Coda the whole thing with a step-by-step of last night's activities at Shoe City and room 110 of the Mesa View.

Payback. Sweet and to the point.

Jimmy's played his closing lines a hundred times over in his head during the course of the morning. *Right where you live, Richard. That's where I set up camp. I walked into Frontier Cleaners and took your money. Then I fucked your wife. And you can't do anything about either.*

Jimmy's got his index finger crooked on the handle of the mailbox. All he has to do is pull it back and drop the envelope in.

Except he doesn't.

He can't.

He's this close, but he can't.

A dog noses up to the corner, circles Jimmy a couple of times, sniffs at his shoes. Its coat looks like a scorched piece of Astroturf. There's nothing warm or doglike about the eyes. They're just eyes. Part of one of its ears is missing.

Jimmy looks back down the block toward the Laundromat, then across the street toward the Southern Pacific rail lines, then farther south, through the haze all the way to the dark rumpled silhouette of the South Mountains.

If only she'd acted guilty, Jimmy thinks, then he could drop the envelope in the mouth of the mailbox and whistle his way back to the spin cycle at the mat. If only before she left his bed for home she had panicked, started crying, done the hysterics, begged him not to tell Richard, had a grand attack of hypocrisy that she'd tried to pass off as conscience; if only she had gone melodramatic on him, sobs and wails and tear-choked pleas, or even tried to shell-game him with a few brazen threats, done the Scottsdale Shuffle, parading the power of social position, the escape hatches of privilege, making sure he understood what the Haves have always had at their disposal; if only she had done any of that, Jimmy could have gone after Richard both barrels and no prisoners.

But the thing is, she hadn't.

She stood naked by the bed, her clothes in a heap, and asked Jimmy if he'd seen her panties. He'd said no. Evelyn had looked around, then shrugged and laughed.

It's that laugh he keeps hearing, deep and throaty, no false bottoms to it.

A laugh like that, it's the equivalent of an endangered species.

Jimmy drops his hand from the handle of the mail slot.

He starts back to the mat. The majority of the storefronts are boarded up or covered with a tic-tac-toe board of iron grillwork, but Jimmy catches enough glimpses of himself in passing windows to disqualify himself as anything approaching dapper. He'd forgotten to shave this morning, and despite some hairbrush action, his scalp's sporting the sea-urchin look, but the most unfortunate side effect of his decision to wash everything he owned was his choice of interim wardrobe—in this case, the baggy shorts he'd fashioned from an old pair of jeans, Jimmy a little off with the scissor work so that the left leg ended up three inches shorter than the right, a pair of Force One athletic shoes he'd set aside from the Shoe City job, their seams already splitting and most of the color leached away, and a white T-shirt with the Batman logo emblazoned across the chest, the shirt passed down from Don Ruger's oldest son when his enthusiasm for the Caped Crusader waned, the shirt itself a victim of too many launderings, having shrunk to the fit of a tourniquet, the sleeves pulling up and riding the top of his shoulders and bisecting his armpits.

His clothes have just kicked into final spin when Jimmy gets back to the Laundromat. The load in one of the machines has shifted, throwing the washer off balance, and it bounces and strains against the brackets holding it in place, sounding like an engine about to throw a rod.

Jimmy tosses the manila envelope on the seat of the first chair inside the door and then crosses to the washer, hopping up and perching on the lip of its lid, his teeth and bones rattling as he rides out the cycle.

Jimmy's thinking maybe it's time to pick up a case of thirty-weight and a half dozen pints of tranny fluid and point the Beast northwest and head for Montana. Leon Glade, the tender at the Chute, has a vet buddy who owns a bar in Helena, and Jimmy's pretty sure he could land some straight-time work there.

He's crossed the bridge to thirty-five, and lately every one of the ideas that have hatched a plan seem more and more like one of those plug-in air fresheners, sweet-smelling when you first take it out of the box but that always turns out to have the life span of a fruit fly, and before you know it, you're left with a small, empty plastic cage stuck in a light socket and you're breathing the same old air.

Jimmy's had four dryers cranked for twenty minutes when Aaron Limbe and Newt Deems show up.

Jimmy looks around the mat. There's one other person in the place, an older woman with long black hair shotgunned with gray streaks sitting along the east wall. Aaron Limbe stands just inside the door wearing what looks like a defrocked Boy Scout's uniform, a plain tan work shirt and matching tan pants. His shoes are shined, and the part in his short black hair looks razored.

Newt Deems walks over to the older woman sitting along the east wall. He takes a buck from the pocket of his jeans and holds it out to her. Newt mentions the diner a couple doors down, tells her it might be a good idea to get herself a cup of coffee.

"We'll make sure nobody bothers your clothes," he adds.

Jimmy watches Aaron Limbe unwrap a breath mint and slip it in his mouth.

The older woman slowly gets up and walks out without a word. Newt shrugs, takes the buck over to the soft drink machine, and punches out a Mountain Dew. The tarantula tattoo covering the back of his hand flexes when the can disappears into his palm. Newt finishes the drink off in two swallows. When he turns toward Jimmy, Newt blocks out most of the light coming through the east window.

"We're tuned to the same station today, right?" Newt crumples the can and tosses it in the corner.

Jimmy nods.

"Good." Newt walks over to where Jimmy's leaning against the folding tables. "I collect, we're gone."

"I told Ray I'd drop the money off at six," Jimmy says.

"Something came up," Newt says. "The Mexican thing again. Limon Perez keeps riling up the other gangs. Ray's set up a powwow."

From across the room, Aaron Limbe laughs. It's as flat and empty as a slow clap. "Perez understands one thing," he says, "and it's not talk. He's like you that way, Coates."

Newt waves him off. "I want the money. We gotta book."

"I'm busy right now," Jimmy says.

Newt looks down at the floor for a moment and begins balling his fists. "You got what you owe or not, Jimmy?"

"I do, but not here. Ray said six o'clock."

"We'll go get it then. Come on." Newt turns toward the door.

"I told you I'm busy." Jimmy points at the wall of dryers, the tumble of clothes behind their glass faces.

Newt grabs Jimmy by the back of the neck and pins his head sideways on the folding table, Jimmy getting a close-up of the contact paper's yellow-and-white-checkered print, scorch marks from mislaid cigarettes, stained ovals from the bottom of soft drink cans, and a line of black ants, all of them swimming in and out of focus as Newt applies more pressure. It feels like there's a car resting on his neck.

Jimmy's left arm's free, flailing around, and it hits Newt's belt and the buck knife he carries around with him. Jimmy fumbles with the clasp on the sheath and gets his hand on the knife, but when it's out, he can't do anything with it, the angle of his arm all wrong, and Jimmy ends up just waving the knife in the air by his own leg.

Newt takes the knife from him and then leans over and edges the bottom of Jimmy's earlobe, slicing the skin off its tip. He drops a thin peel of flesh on the table. It looks like the rind on a piece of bologna.

Newt steps back, and Jimmy's up, hyperventilating and coughing at the same time. His chest feels like it's packed with sand. He touches the side of his neck, and his fingertips come away red.

The dryers buzz and then cut off.

Jimmy stumbles over and starts unloading them, gathering great draping armfuls that he then drops on the folding table.

"I'm not believing this," Newt says.

Aaron Limbe walks over and takes out his gun.

He points the .38 at Jimmy's chest. There's nothing recognizable in Limbe's eyes.

Jimmy wipes his hand on the back of his cut-offs and begins sorting and folding.

"What in hell's wrong with you?" Newt asks. "I don't get it. You want to die over four loads of laundry?"

There's a point where there isn't one anymore, Jimmy thinks. You just have had enough. You're tired of people jamming you up. You torch common sense, leave reason in the dust. You're beyond appeal. You're suddenly willing to die for God, country, or four loads of laundry. It's not something you think about. You're there, that's all, simply there, right in the middle of it.

And for no reason that makes any sense, you feel damn good.

"You want the money," Jimmy says, pointing at the table, "you help me fold these first."

Newt takes a step back and tells Aaron Limbe, "Fuck this. Shoot him."

Ray Harp pounds on the door and then steps inside. As usual, he's wearing a blue three-piece suit, cowboy boots, and no shirt. He asks what's taking so long.

Newt explains the situation. Ray looks over at Limbe and Jimmy. Limbe still has the .38 pointed at Jimmy's chest.

"Let me get this straight," Ray says. "Newt's just cut off part of your ear and told Aaron to shoot you because before I get what you owe me, you want them to help you fold your laundry?"

Jimmy nods. "Those are my terms."

"Oh man," Ray says, shaking his head. "You are one piece of work." Ray then dredges up a laugh from his biker days, one with an arbitrary and unexpected reprieve built into it.

Ray waves Newt Deems and Aaron Limbe over to the table and tells them to get started.

"You serious?" Newt asks. "We're going along with this bullshit?"

"Start folding," Ray says. He wanders over to the chairs lining the front window and sits down.

Limbe is slow in lowering the pistol. "I'm not going to forget this."

Jimmy whistles "La Cucaracha" as he divides the sprawling pile of clothes into thirds. The left shoulder of the Batman T-shirt is spackled in red, but the bleeding from his ear has almost stopped.

There's a hiss like Scotch tape being pulled up each time one of them grabs a piece of laundry. "Static cling," Jimmy says, "ain't it a bitch?"

Aaron Limbe works as methodically on the pile before him as a buzzard over a piece of carrion. Newt's handling his like a short-order cook with a faulty memory.

Jimmy treats them to another round of "La Cucaracha."

As they finish up and put the folded clothes in the black plastic trash bags, Ray Harp calls out from across the room, "You know, Jimmy, if the money's not there I'm handing you over to Aaron and Newt here, and before they kill you, you'll wish your grandfather had never been born. That's how bad they're going to hurt you. We're talking major DNA violation."

They load the laundry in the backseat of Harp's white Continental and drive to the Mesa View, Newt following in his orange El Camino. Ray's got some early Aerosmith cranked up on the CD player.

"Real nice digs," he says when Jimmy opens the door to 110.

Jimmy walks across the room and kneels before the mini-refrigerator, dragging out a twelve-pack of Milwaukee's Best. He takes out a couple of cans, then slides his hand inside and pulls free the white envelope he's taped to the underside of the top of the box.

Jimmy counts out this week's meet, then hesitates. The envelope's crammed with cash from the dry-cleaning robberies and the thousand from the Shoe City job. He pulls out a wad of bills and counts out what he owes Ray. The whole enchilada. He gathers the cash from the floor and then stands up.

"We're a hundred percent clear now," he says, "so why don't you and those two assholes get out of my room?"

"Manners," Ray says. "Remember your manners." He counts out the money and then slips it in the right-hand inside pocket of his blue suit, looks around the room once more, and then walks out.

Newt Deems hangs back for a moment, his thick features glacially moving into a frown. "I don't get it. The whole time you had the money. Why'd you make me cut you?"

"I'll tell you why," Aaron Limbe says. "Same reason a bird will fly into a window. There are some people who are just too goddamn stupid to tell the difference between glass and air. They never see what's coming. They're defective."

After they leave, Jimmy starts to open a beer and then remembers the envelope with Evelyn's panties. He'd left it back at the Laundromat on the seat of the first chair fronting the window just inside the door.

Jimmy humps it the two long blocks in his Force Ones. The sidewalk's on broil, and the shoes are as unforgiving as pieces of cardboard.

The envelope's gone.

Jimmy can't find it anywhere. He goes through the mat twice.

The woman is back. She's sitting along the east wall near the dryers. Jimmy asks her if she's seen the envelope, adding some fish-story visual aids, pantomiming its width and length.

The woman flat-lines him. No response at all. Won't even look at him.

Jimmy tries again, tells her it's important.

Same deal. On one level, Jimmy's relieved because the woman's expression shows no sign at all of any impulse toward a Good Samaritan number. Odds are if the woman or anyone else in the neighborhood found the envelope, they'd check it for cash and then toss it, not dutifully walk it to the corner and drop it in the mailbox.

Jimmy circles the mat, once more, for a last check.

"About twenty-five minutes ago," the woman says. Her voice reminds Jimmy of someone snapping kindling. Jimmy doesn't turn around. He waits until the woman goes on to say that's when someone came through and picked up the trash.

"It's in a dumpster out back," she adds. "Help yourself."

Jimmy's not sure if she's referring to the manila envelope in particular or the trash in general, but when he walks back behind the mat and sees the fly action around the overflowing dumpster, he decides it's a moot point. No way he's rooting around in that buzz.

Back at the Mesa View Inn, he grabs two beers, setting one on the bathroom sink and taking the other into the shower with him. He stays until the hot water runs out, then dries off and goes to work on his ear, dousing the cut with peroxide and wrapping the outer edge of the lobe with Band-Aids. He palms four aspirin and washes them down with the second beer.

Tired as he is, his mood's jump-started when it finally sinks in he's clear of Ray Harp. No more looking over his shoulder. No more interest-choked deadlines. He's clear.

Jimmy figures it's time to swing by the Chute for a little "reversal of fortune" celebration.

He digs out a pair of jeans and fresh shirt from the laundry bag and finishes dressing. From out in the lot are two short taps of a car horn.

A few moments later, the same thing.

Jimmy steps through the door.

At first all he sees is the blinding sun-glazed curve of a windshield, and then Evelyn tilts her head outside its frame. She has the engine running and the radio on. The wind has bird-nested her hair. She's wearing large silver hoop earrings, and her lipstick's the same shade of red as the Mustang.

"Three days," she says. "He'll be gone three days."

EIGHTEEN

They're not in the house more than fifteen minutes before they end up in the bedroom.

Evelyn's surprised at how easy it is for her to tell Jimmy what she wants.

She's surprised, too, at how easy it had been to step out of her life, the boundaries of who she'd been. It hadn't seemed possible before. Evelyn had always seen herself and others as weighted to the world and their lives, heavy with the obligations of character.

Evelyn had always been good at that, keeping things from getting out of hand. Taking care of her father after her mother left, running the household at thirteen, the schoolteacher's daughter who understood the requirements of duty; the good student who understood the requirements of hard work; the young wife who understood the requirements of sacrifice; the flight attendant who understood the requirements of civility and comfort; the friend, neighbor, and citizen who understood the requirements of living within the lines of whatever was expected of her.

The blinds on the bedroom windows are open. Evelyn reaches to close them, then drops her arm. She likes the slant of the afternoon light, the way it reaches and fills the room.

Jimmy's standing next to the bed.

Evelyn walks over and unbuttons his shirt.

She is coming to understand something: Desire leaves no room for facts. Suddenly she is not thinking about the fact that she's about to sleep with her brother-in-law, or about the fact that she forgot to call Linda and Marie and cancel their luncheon date, or the fact that her husband will be home in sixty-eight hours. The facts may feel solid, but if she holds them up to the light, she can see right through them.

Desire, she's coming to discover, leaves no room for anything but itself.

There's a slight tremor in her hands as she fingers the buttons on Jimmy's shirt, the same tremor she's felt on her afternoon drives in the desert, a trembling that runs through her legs and arms and trips the nerve endings along her spine, opening up something she can't put a name to, filling and pressing against her insides like an umbrella suddenly torn open by an abrupt gust of wind.

They fall into bed, and there's a long moment just before they touch when anything seems possible, when the world has disappeared into waiting flesh.

Everything stops and starts with that first touch.

"Yes," Evelyn says, lifting her hips.

There's fit and need, nothing else, and it's sweet and lovely, oh so lovely, and Evelyn thrusts and follows the rush of her pulse, living in her blood, chasing a place where words falter, then break down, and the names of things become unmoored, a point where sex cleanses you of language and you simply inhabit the crush of breath and flesh and leave your name behind.

"Hope you're hungry," Jimmy says. He's standing at the kitchen counter, three eggs wedged between index and middle fingers, middle and ring fingers, and ring and pinkie. He drops his hand, turning the wrist at the last moment so that the eggs catch the edge of the blue mixing bowl with a quick simultaneous crack. Jimmy lifts his arm straight up at the moment of contact, the whites and yolks making a three-point landing in the bottom of the bowl.

He adds three more eggs to the bowl and then ransacks the shelves of the fridge. He's mixing up his specialty, what he calls Junkyard Omelettes, and anything's fair game: a couple jalapenos, some onion, a few chunks of cheddar, a dash of barbeque sauce, cup of milk, a handful of leftover chicken pieces, and a half can of beer.

Jimmy looks over his shoulder at Evelyn. She's sitting on the sill of the bay window of the breakfast nook painting her toenails. She hasn't bothered with clothes. In the slant of the day's light, her skin's as pale as a slice of bread.

"Neighbors," Jimmy says. "You're presenting an eyeful there, Evelyn, anybody'd care to snoop."

"I don't care. The light's nice here." She takes the brush through tiny, brightly colored maneuvers.

Before turning back to the counter, Jimmy takes one more look at Evelyn, at the tight bow her body makes when she bends over with the brush.

He's not ready for what he's seen.

Evelyn might have been messing around, vamping it up on the windowsill there, doing some sex-pot or vixen number, but it had backfired on her. She looked beautiful instead.

And the fact that she didn't seem aware of looking beautiful just made its effect that much stronger.

Jimmy moves over to the range. He's got the skillet popping, and two chunks of butter chasing each other around the Teflon when he dumps in the contents of the blue bowl and starts charming the eggs with a wooden spoon.

He's trying to match the woman across the room to the one who's married to his brother.

He's not exactly sure if he can or not and if that's a good or bad sign.

Right now, though, it doesn't matter.

At this particular tick of the clock, Jimmy's slotted. Things are looking good. Suddenly hope doesn't feel like another name for a new mistake. There's no need to check the pulse on his prospects today. He's got an empty stomach and breakfast swimming in the skillet, half a cold beer at his elbow, and across the room, a good-looking naked woman painting her nails in the late morning light.

Jimmy tips the skillet and coaxes the eggs onto two white stoneware plates and delivers them up.

She turned her head.

Evelyn remembers standing behind the farmhouse on Dobbins, the smell of brittlebush, sage, mesquite, and baked earth, the sunlight glinting off the bottles and cans set among the small pale fruit in the stunted branches of the orange and lemon trees, and the pull of the T-shirt across her rib cage when she lifted the Diamondback, aimed, and fired, and then slowly let out her breath and smiled, turning her head and finding Jimmy right there.

Evelyn returns to that moment each time she begins thinking about what she's doing and what she's done, and the recriminations start aligning themselves like iron filings under a magnet.

When she starts telling herself it's gone far enough.

She had turned her head, and he was right there.

She can stop things where they are and step back into her life. Chalk up what's happened to folly. Bad judgment. A momentary weakness. Explain it away.

Evelyn can explain everything away, except the kiss.

That's the moment she keeps returning to.

There are kisses that go deeper than marrow. A type of kiss that others can easily mock or sentimentalize, but Evelyn knows better.

You turn your head, and it happens.

A certain type of kiss that refuses to end when it should have, and it scares you.

That's why she had stepped away from Jimmy and said, *I'll decide if that happened or not.*

She had been scared.

Scared of the kiss and what it made her feel. And scared it would never happen again.

• • •

Evelyn's behind the wet bar, fixing them drinks. She lines up glasses, scoops out ice. She's generous with the bourbon, lazy on the water.

She hands Jimmy his drink, then leans in and kisses him, softly at first, then harder.

"You didn't close your eyes this time," she says.

"Evelyn," Jimmy says, but gets no further than her name, because the phone rings and continues to ring until the machine picks it up. Richard's disembodied voice fills every corner of the silence.

They listen to Richard remind her that he'll be coming in tomorrow afternoon and give her the time, airline, and flight number and then tell her that he's missed her.

Jimmy turns and walks out of the room.

She finds him in the kitchen standing over the answering machine.

He looks over his shoulder at her, then hits the Play button.

Richard's voice surrounds them once again.

Evelyn raises her hand. "Jimmy, please."

The message has barely finished when, again, Jimmy hits Rewind, then Play.

Evelyn hears her husband's voice, even-toned, the words carefully measured, and she feels the slow pull of the old orbit of self, the gravitational field of a marriage.

When the machine clicks and the red light begins blinking, she crosses the room and presses Erase.

"That simple, huh?" Jimmy says.

"Is that what you think, Jimmy? That any of this is easy for me?"

"I don't know," he says. "Is it?" He takes a long swallow of his drink and then lowers the glass. "I mean, how hard exactly is it to take a little vacation from being Mrs. Richard Coates?"

"Don't do this, Jimmy. Not tonight."

"You didn't answer the question, Evelyn."

She lets out her breath and looks away. Outside the bay window, there's a fat dollop of yellow moon and a salting of stars over Camelback Mountain. Evelyn leans over and undoes the straps on her shoes, then slowly levers each off, toes to heel, and leaves them in the middle of the kitchen floor.

"Let's go upstairs, Jimmy," she says.

The crime lab people would have a field day if they dusted the place.

It's 3:00 A.M., and Jimmy, barefoot and in jeans, unable to sleep, is downstairs, moving around his brother's house. It's a big place, a two-and-a-half-story, with a long steeply sloping roof, its exterior a mortared wall of light gray rocks of different sizes and shapes set at angles to each other, like a landslide that's been arrested midfall. Inside, the rooms are wide and airy, the ceilings crosshatched with dark exposed beams.

Jimmy wants to make his presence felt. He passed on the idea of taking something from the house, settling instead on making whatever lay within an arm's reach his. He's leaving his prints on every available surface, touching everything, imprinting himself on his brother's life and possessions, hoping to subtract something each time his fingers make contact.

There are Remington prints hanging in the dining room and den. A cavernous fireplace whose mantle is lined with Paiute and Tohono O'odham woven baskets interspersed with kachina dolls. Hardwood floors with brightly dyed Navajo rugs. A framed territorial map circa 1830. A mahogany gun case. A rack of cowboy hats. Two crossed ceremonial cavalry sabers. A black wire sculpture of a thrashing bronco. A dented tin bucket mounded with silver dollars. Collections of arrowheads mounted behind glass. A horse-hoof ashtray. Immense wagon-wheel chandeliers. Vases, everywhere, filled with dried desert flowers. The furniture, squat and low, upholstered in shades of tan and brown and soft orange.

Richard was a big fan of the fact that their ties to the region went back to the founding of Fort McDowell at the close of the Civil War through the reopening of the original canal system built by the Hohokam tribe. Their great-great-grandfather had been instrumental in stealing the territorial capital from Prescott and getting it moved to Phoenix, and their great-uncle had helped bankroll the commission for the blinding-white angel of mercy statue that eventually stood on the copper dome of the capitol building. Their grandfather and his brood had pulled a lot of heavy-duty political strings when it came to support and funding for the Roosevelt Dam and Salt River Project, and he then went on to make his money in agriculture, primarily cotton and meatpacking, when Phoenix's slaughterhouses were the largest, outside Chicago, in the country. Late in his life, their grandfather subtracted a long line of zeroes from the family fortune when he invested in a series of resort projects lavish enough to make a sultan blush and everything went belly-up shortly after the groundbreakings.

Along the way, Jimmy's ancestors dropped enough coin in the name of art and culture and regional heritage to qualify as the Valley of the Sun's version of solid citizens, and that's the part Richard loves and plays to with his country club pals and chamber of commerce buddies.

Jimmy eventually moves to the kitchen. It's going on 4:00 A.M. Hanging near the phone is a wooden key chain. He spots the letters *RC* on one of the sets, snags it, and walks through an enclosed breezeway and into the garage.

He gets behind the wheel of his brother's silver Lexus.

His brother's got a system of shelves and wall hangings so that all the tools and hardware are ordered and in place, and Jimmy feels like he's back on some grade school field trip, the teacher lining them up in front of a museum display that contains a lesson for their own good.

The garage is easily three times the size of his room at the Mesa View.

Jimmy's suddenly thinking grand theft auto and arson. Sitting along the base of the north wall of the garage are five gallons of high-test unleaded in a squat red plastic container.

He fingers the pack of matches in his shirt pocket.

He's considering taking the unleaded and burning his initials in the front lawn, a little signature work, twenty-foot letters charred in the St. Augustine grass like a brand.

Then maybe take the Lexus over to Pete Samoa's and negotiate some chop-shop action and pocket the take.

Jimmy slots the key in the ignition and then reaches up for the door opener clipped to the visor and does an open sesame, the garage door slowly coming to life, rumbling and clanking on its tracks.

He keeps running through the various combos of crimes against property, and they're all holding TRY ME signs, but he's jammed up. They all fit and simultaneously fall short of what he's feeling. His brother's got to pay, but Jimmy can't settle on the right amount.

Evelyn keeps getting in the way.

He could have mailed Evelyn's panties to Richard and finished things right there. He could have ignored the message Richard left on the answering machine. But he didn't do either. Or couldn't. A jump ball on that one.

The garage door clicks to a stop. Jimmy's looking at a rectangle of driveway and lawn swimming in moonlight.

Scottsdale itself is part of the problem, with its country clubs and golf courses and art galleries and upscale boutiques and quaint restaurants and resort complexes, and there's the Lexus he's sitting in and the wedding cake landscaping and the big stone monument that Richard calls home, everywhere the presence of money and the truths it can buy so that even the air feels different, as if it has been jacked up a couple of extra molecules.

Richard wakes up to all of this every day. It's his. Jimmy will never be able to touch it.

There's a power in the right address and zip code that rivals any threat Ray Harp can level at you.

And then Jimmy's back to thinking about Evelyn again.

And when he pulls the keys from the ignition and points the remote and watches the door accordion itself to a close, he's thinking about how over the years he's been accused of thinking with his feet or of thinking with his dick; and as he climbs out of the car and walks back into the house and heads for the stairway that will take him to the master bedroom and the woman who'd bushwhacked him earlier with her beauty, he's starting to wonder just what part of him is doing the thinking now.

Evelyn's lying on her side, propped on an elbow. The sheets have slipped to the rounded curve of a hip. Her hair's falling in her eyes, and she's practicing a pout, the sexy kind that Jimmy always associates with French women, though he's not sure exactly why, since he's never met one.

"You were talking in your sleep," she says.

Jimmy lifts his head from the pillow. Across the room, morning's burning in the window. He remembers sitting behind the wheel of his brother's silver Lexus, coming back into the house and having a couple of drinks, but beyond that, nothing.

"Who's Debbie?" Evelyn asks, pinching him. "A rival for my affections?"

Jimmy frowns, then shakes his head. "Mystery woman. Can't place the name or the dream."

"You sure?" Evelyn's smiling, her hand slipping under the sheets and moving south. "You sounded a little lovesick, Jimmy."

The fingers of the hand she's slipped between his legs have turned into tiny bustling hives, and suddenly the name's there.

"Debbie Greene," Jimmy says.

He laughs, looks over at Evelyn, and then jump-cuts to the fifth grade. He tells her about his first official boner. Not the generalized or unfocused boners that came from the texture of flannel pajamas or the chaos of wet dreams, but a boner with a point, though one that Jimmy only dimly understood at the time, sitting with his opened lunchbox in the school cafeteria a table over from Debbie Greene and her wild red hair punctuated with yellow butterfly barrettes. Jimmy had been sitting with Don Ruger and Larry Talbert and unsuccessfully trying to cut a deal involving Cheetos and bologna sandwiches when he saw her glance his way. Once, just once.

But it had been enough.

Jimmy felt the sudden confusion in his jeans as the deal for the Cheetos fell through and Debbie Greene sat giggling with her friends a table over, Jimmy taking an orange out of his lunchbox and beginning to peel it, slipping his finger under the rounded navel, the skin giving away, his fingers finding pulp and juice, the smell of the orange mixing with the smell of warm milk from the small waxy container setting next to his elbow.

The boner had still been tenting the front of his pants when lunch period ended, Mrs. Lidd, his fifth-grade teacher, coming over and getting on his case about finishing on time, Jimmy not wanting to get up from the seat, Debbie Greene and her friends walking by and giggling as they got in line, Mrs. Lidd hovering over him, Jimmy slipping a piece of the orange peel in his shirt pocket as his boner reluctantly subsided and Mrs. Lidd loudly cataloged the various problems Jimmy had in the attitude and discipline departments and made dire predictions about his suitability as a future citizen of the republic.

Evelyn laughs and asks what happened to her.

"Mrs. Lidd?"

"No," she says, still laughing. "The girl with the butterfly barrettes."

"Oh," Jimmy says. "I only saw her a couple of times after that. Her old man was a manager at the Motorola plant in Chandler and they transferred him out. I think Denver."

Evelyn doesn't have anything to say to that, and in the silence that suddenly crops up between them, Jimmy finds that he doesn't either.

NINETEEN

There's a lopsided moon outside the kitchen window and a stillness to the night, a kind of space between breaths, that reminds Aaron Limbe of his stint in Nicaragua.

Six years in the army, the last four in Special Forces, then twelve years on the Phoenix PD, the last seventeen months working for Ray Harp, all of it leading up to where he is standing now, in the kitchen of his childhood home, a tilted quarter moon in the window, and Aaron Limbe holding an eight-by-ten of Evelyn Coates in a white half-slip, one bra strap loose and slipping over her shoulder, her head tilted so that her hair swings free, as she leans into the kiss from Jimmy Coates.

Coates, shirtless, has his hand resting against her neck.

Aaron Limbe carries the photo from the kitchen through a small foyer leading off to the front door and into the living room. He adds the photo to the others. Thumbtacked on its north wall in precise floor-to-ceiling rows are seventy-two black-and-white photographs of Coates and his sister-in-law.

He then walks down the hall toward his bedroom, his footsteps echoing in the narrow space, the light dim from the single ceiling fixture.

Limbe pulls a black footlocker from under his bed and, with effort, carries it back to the kitchen.

He works the combination and takes out a Marlin .45

semi-automatic rifle, a Sig Sauer P239, a Charter Arms revolver, and Taurus auto-pistol and places them on the kitchen table. He then sorts through the locker matching ammo to each. He dismantles the guns one at a time and starts cleaning them.

The phone rings. Limbe has disconnected his answering machine, and he lets the phone ring itself out.

Limbe swabs out the barrel of the rifle and then attaches a night scope. At his left elbow is a compact pyramid of stacked ammo boxes.

Aaron Limbe is coming to judgment.

The waiting's over.

Limbe has waited, because that's what he's learned, the true weight of time when you placed it on the scales and waited for them to right themselves and balance.

He is approaching an absolute and true clarity, the same kind he found in the middle of the night in a small cement block room in a nondescript building on the far western outskirts of Managua. It was the kind of clarity only an interrogation room could produce.

Aaron Limbe knows this: Tie someone to a chair in a bare room, and with enough time and enough questions, you eventually come down to one essential truth—every heart is a crime scene.

Limbe finishes cleaning the Marlin semiautomatic and starts on the Sig Sauer and Charter Arms.

The phone again. Sixteen rings before it cuts off. Two more than last time.

Above the house is the low rumble of an F-15 making its approach to Luke Air Force Base.

If he closes his eyes, he can see the exact sequence of photos he's thumbtacked to the north wall of the living room, eight rows down and nine shots per row, seventy-two black-and-whites of Coates and his sister-in-law doing what his master sergeant had called the Gland Dance.

Limbe massages the back of his neck. That's where they always start, the headaches, just below the base of his skull.

Gathering the evidence had not been difficult. Coates and his sister-in-law were as predictable as lab rats. After some of the reconnaissance work he'd done in Nicaragua, tracking two amateur adulterers obsessed with each other's orifices hadn't been a stretch. They didn't see Limbe, because they weren't looking for him. He's been following them for over a month and a half now.

Limbe sets down the Charter Arms and picks up the Taurus. It's one of two throw-down guns he's kept from his time on the police force. The Taurus is light, just a little over twelve ounces with a nine-shot .22-long magazine, and easily concealed and therefore handy in tight or unexpected situations.

Within the next three days, he will kill Jimmy Coates.

He's waited patiently, very patiently, for two conditions to manifest themselves. One is that Jimmy Coates must not see his death coming. It must be totally unexpected, something he cannot prepare for or prevent. The second condition was trickier. His death must rob Coates of something important. Coates had to die right at the point where he'd found something that mattered to him.

His death, in other words, had to duplicate what he'd done to Aaron Limbe when Coates had cut the deal with the police brass, claiming he could put Limbe and Ramon Delgado together the night of the safe-house fire, and Limbe had been forced to resign from the force.

With a loser like Coates, the first condition had been easy from the start. Coates had never been able to see anything coming. His whole life was a testament to faulty wiring. The second condition was another story. From what Aaron Limbe could see, Jimmy Coates had the complexity of an amoeba. Everything about his life was insignificant. Nothing had ever mattered to him.

Nothing, that is, until the sister-in-law. The last six weeks have proven that.

When he's done cleaning the weapons, Limbe wraps each in a piece of cloth and returns them to the footlocker.

He drinks two more glasses of water, then leans against the

sink and closes his eyes. He feels a great still point taking shape within him.

He's been dreaming Nicaragua.

There was a drain in the center of the floor.

The cement block walls had been painted with lime and were always damp.

A thing is what it's named.

Insurgents, for instance. Rebels.

You asked the questions, and after a while, you were in the mouth of God.

Every death is a lesson.

There were women, locals, who came in and cleaned up afterward.

Within that interrogation room, Aaron Limbe rediscovered what he'd always known: There are only two worlds, the true world and the fallen world, and in the true world everything has its true shape and true fit, which form and complete the true universal hierarchy, which is forever and untouched by history.

In the fallen world, there is no clarity, and a thing cannot recognize its own shape. The fallen world is bloat and buzz and everywhere form without purpose.

The phone starts in again. Limbe takes his time answering it. He knows who it is.

"Aaron?" Ray Harp asks. "Where in the hell have you been?"

Limbe enjoys the mix of anger and panic in Harp's voice.

"What do you want, Ray?"

"I want you over here. As in an hour and a half ago. I want you watching my back." He pauses. "One of Limon Perez's boys shot Newt Deems. He's alive and in one of those ICU places, but it doesn't look good."

"I told you trusting Perez was a mistake."

"If he's happy," Ray says, "the other Mexican gangs go along. They look up to him. We negotiated. Perez wanted a larger cut of the action. The way I figured it, there's enough green to spread around, so I said okay. Next thing I know, Newt's in emergency surgery. It doesn't make any sense."

Packs of hyenas, Limbe thinks, all of them—Ray Harp, his biker pals, the Mex crank gangs. All of them, nothing more than teeth and fur and the smell of blood in the air.

"I got the word out to my brothers," Harp says. "If Newt dies, we're going to hit Perez hard. Make a counterstatement. I'll need you to coordinate things."

"You waited too long, Ray," Limbe says. "You should have let me take out Perez six months ago."

"Just get over here."

"I don't think so," Limbe says.

"Quit dicking around. You heard what I said."

"You keep them in their place, Ray," Limbe says. "You show them their place, then you put them in it and you keep them there. It doesn't matter if it's taco-benders or niggers or losers like Coates. You don't negotiate with them. You draw lines. You hold those lines. That's all they understand."

"Listen to me," Ray says. "I figure I'm going to need some round-the-clock here until we see how things play out. I want to be ready this time."

"You're already speaking from the grave, Ray," Limbe says. "It's over. Limon Perez won't stop now. You had your chance." He pauses, then adds, "You're done. And I'm out."

"What's this shit, out? You work for me."

"Not anymore."

Harp's laugh sounds more like a bark. "Who do you think's going to take you on? You're a sick motherfucker, Limbe. I gave you a place. No one else will. You're too fucked up."

Limbe has no time for the welter of appetites governed by biker logic that Harp calls a life. He hangs up the phone.

Then he takes a deep breath and rips the whole unit out of the wall.

Aaron Limbe knows this: He is coming to judgment. He is untouchable.

He walks down the hall and unlocks the door to his mother's bedroom. He's converted it into a darkroom, and hanging on a thin wire above the pans of developing solution are nine black-and-white shots—reprints of the center row of photographs on the living-room wall. He checks to see if they're dry and then takes them down and carries them back to the kitchen and sets them on the table in front of his chair.

He looks over at the pale rectangle between the refrigerator and calendar where the phone had hung.

Then Aaron Limbe hunts down his Exacto knife and returns to the kitchen table.

TWENTY

"Hey, Leon," Jimmy says, "you got a problem with your hearing? A little wax buildup maybe, something along those lines?"

"You want another?"

"I do," Jimmy says, "but that's not what I was asking you."

He watches Leon rack down a new glass and tilt it against the draft spout, four inches of churning foam running and rising to its lip.

The fact that Leon's got a new pair of glasses hasn't improved his skill as a bartender. He sets the draft in front of Jimmy and goes back to work on the model airplane he's got spread across a sheet of newspaper on the bar top.

Leon's turned the inside of the Chute into a regular air show. Suspended from the ceiling at varying heights are scale models of bomber and pursuit planes, a floating arsenal of Bearcats and Mustangs and Spitfires and P-47s and 51s and B-17s and 29s slowly bobbing under the ceiling fans like a horde of oversized exotic insects. Leon's even got one hanging in the crapper, a fat submarine-sandwich-sized B-24.

"Don Ruger was in earlier looking for you," Leon says. "I'm not sure if I told you that or not."

"You did," Jimmy says. "Now you can add memory loss to your hearing problems."

"He said it was important," Leon adds.

A few stools down a couple of the regulars start launching peanuts at the aquarium tank holding the sidewinder. The snake, thick as Jimmy's forearm, lifts its head and strikes the glass twice.

"Hey, Gene, knock it off, okay?" Leon says. "The snake's mean enough as it is."

"Wasn't me. Pete was shooting the nuts."

"Don't care which one of you's doing it. Just stop it." Leon points down the bar with part of a P-38 tail section.

"You got no sense of humor, Leon," Pete says. "That's a real liability in a bartender."

"Speaking of which," Gene says, "you hear the one about the two cowboys decided to become bounty hunters?"

Jimmy waves him off. "Not right now, Gene. Leon and I were having a conversation."

"Tell it or not," Pete says, "Leon won't laugh. He's like that wooden Indian in the Hank Williams song. You know, 'Poor Old Caligula.' "

"That was a titty movie with Romans," Gene says. "Remember? We watched it on Cinemax After-Hours."

Jimmy keeps trying to get Leon's attention and the conversation back on track, but Leon's hunkered over the bar, working on matching the seams in the tail section of the P-38.

Jimmy finally reaches over and lightly taps Leon on the shoulder. Leon starts, and his thumb slips. There's a tiny plastic snap, and then a piece of the tail section's dangling.

Leon curses and stomps off for a fresh tube of epoxy and more toothpicks.

Pete gets up and heads off to the men's room.

Gene slides down a couple of stools. He's got a gray crew cut, six Slim Jims marshalling the breast pocket of his shirt, and a rough red rash covering his wrists and forearms. He and Pete work for an exterminating outfit, and they're a little lax with the gloves and masks when they're spraying.

"This one'll kill you, Jimmy," Gene says. "See, you got two

hard-luck cowboys named Toby and Earl. They've done a little of everything, but it's tough times and they're broke. Can't get a job. Then they hook up with this guy tells them he'll pay six dollars for every Indian scalp they bring in."

"I think I've heard this one," Jimmy says, but Gene won't give it up. He rattles through Toby's and Earl's new career as bounty hunters. The first time out they surprise a hunting party of Comanches and are forty-eight bucks to the good. The next time they scalp six. The time after that, twelve. They're doing pretty well and thinking about branching out to Apaches.

"So Toby and Earl, they've been tracking this band of Indians for five days," Gene says, "and they're ready to make their move. They set up camp at the base of this bluff and turn in for a good night's sleep."

"Okay," Jimmy says. "I got the picture."

"Anyway," Gene says, unwrapping a Slim Jim, "the next morning Toby's the first one up. He opens the tent flap and steps out, and what he sees is Indians everywhere. Toby and him are surrounded. Thousands of Indians, one horizon to the other. Toby, he just stands there, taking it all in. Then he starts hollering for Earl to wake up."

Gene leans closer, waving the Slim Jim in Jimmy's face. "Toby's dancing around yelling to Earl, 'Take a look at this. We made it, man. The big time. Six bucks a head. WE'RE RICH!'"

Pete comes back from the men's. Gene points out he forgot to zip his pants. Pete reminds Gene they still have one more job, a harvester-ant infestation at an apartment complex in Encanto Park, before they punch out for the day.

Before they leave, Gene tells Jimmy that Don Ruger had been in looking for him earlier.

Leon takes their empty glasses, douses them in the rinse basin, and reracks them. He draws Jimmy another beer without him asking. Jimmy knows that's Leon's way of saying leave him alone.

The problem is, Jimmy can't. He needs to know if Leon's talked to his buddy in Montana. The guy owns a bar, and Leon was supposed to put a word in for Jimmy about a job.

A regular one, strictly straight-time.

Jimmy's trying to work something out, and that's how he needs to play it. He can't afford to screw this one up.

He raps twice softly on the bar top. "You know, Leon, you never got around to telling me what I was asking you about earlier," Jimmy says. "You know, if you talked to Frank Dawson."

"Lawson," Leon says without looking up. "His name's Lawson." Leon dips the tip of the toothpick in a small puddle of epoxy he's laid out on the newspaper and starts edging the cracked seam in the tail of the P-38.

"Back to the original subject—you told me you were going to call him, Leon."

"He's got this chronic thing with stones," Leon says. He dips the toothpick back in the glue. "Been real sick. He won't do the ultrasound thing, you know where they break them up. He waits until he can pass them instead."

"I need that job," Jimmy says.

"You got stones, you don't feel like talking on the telephone."

"Come on, Leon. This is important."

"I'll talk to him when I talk to him," Leon says, setting down the toothpick and cracking his knuckles. "The guy's in real pain."

Right now, Jimmy could say the same thing. He can't quit thinking about Montana. Coattailing that is his sister-in-law, Evelyn. He can't quit thinking about her either. They keep colliding in his head like two bumper cars endlessly tracking each other.

This is what it comes down to: Jimmy's going to steal his brother's wife, and he wants a clean getaway.

It's not payback for his brother finessing him out of his inheritance, not anymore. It's both more simple and more complicated than that.

Jimmy's in love.

There's no other way to put it.

Jimmy's come to recognize the signs.

For one thing, the world's bigger. Jimmy noticed that right away. You fall in love, and the world starts growing on you.

There's suddenly all this space between things. Everything's large. You find you have acres to maneuver.

The flip side to that is what happens to time. Basically, you run out of it. You've suddenly got too much world and not enough clock. Everything's large and nothing's slow.

That's when you tack a map of Montana on the wall of your room in the Mesa View Inn and redline the route straight to Helena.

That's when your days feel like a sock abruptly turned inside out.

That's when thoughts of your sister-in-law's left breast keep popping up in your head, and you can't shut them down. No matter what you're doing, her left breast keeps following you around, and you're thinking of its heft and hang, the way its nipple is like a grape on its way to becoming a raisin when she's aroused.

That's when you end up with pronoun problems, the sudden and stubborn presence of an *us* or *we* in your vocabulary.

And finally, you look at your hands, and that's when you know you're in love, because they're not yours anymore. What you touch, she does. It's like her hands are secreted within yours, and your own hands are over hers, covering them like gloves. Except you can't take them off. That's the catch. You can't separate your touch from hers. Her hands, your hands, they're a perfect fit.

Anything you touch, she's there with you.

And there's nothing you can do about it, absolutely nothing, and that's when you know you've taken the fall, and it's the long one.

TWENTY-ONE

As he crosses Washington and starts for the courtyard fronting the old capitol building, there is a taste, like that of damp earth, that fills his mouth to the back of his throat, and Aaron Limbe unwraps a breath mint and slips it onto his tongue.

Despite the midday heat, he is wearing his dark blue suit. He has a new haircut and carries a slim brown attaché case. His black shoes are buffed to an army-regulation shine.

He passes in front of the old capitol building with its triangular cornice and six columns and tan granite walls, all topped with the massive copper dome and white angel of mercy statue. The building was converted in 1974 into a museum, where the state's history was defanged and hung on the walls or put in glass display cases.

Free admission, Limbe thinks, to all the old lies.

Directly behind the old capitol is the new annex, its central gray facade as blankly rectangular as a wafer set on end.

Inserted between the gridwork of sidewalks are rose and cacti gardens, beds of lantana and impatiens, the quadrants edged with evenly spaced rows of boxwoods and the staggered lines of shaggy-barked palms.

He looks at his watch. The breath mint does nothing to cut the taste in his mouth.

Limbe angles along the eastern edge of the capitol mall past the mounted anchor reclaimed from the USS *Arizona* that had been sunk at Pearl Harbor, then west to Wesley Brolin Plaza, a ten-acre park lying between Fifteenth and Seventeenth Avenues and Adams and Jefferson. At noon, it's full of office-pale government workers, joggers, tourists, rollerbladers, senior citizens, and herds of kids on outings from day-care centers.

Limbe continues west, following a tree-lined walkway until he comes to a fountain being repaired. The workers have taken off on their lunch break. Ten yards away on a wooden park bench is Richard Coates.

When Limbe had worked in the Phoenix PD, no one had wanted next-of-kin duty, his fellow officers going to any lengths to avoid it, constantly pulling rank, calling in markers, cajoling, or outright bribing each other, anything that would let them off the hook. Limbe, though, hadn't minded. In fact, he liked it, enjoyed the ceremony of the routine, the knock on the door, the charged interval before someone finally answered it, when he would take off his cap and tuck it under his arm, square his shoulders, and empty his face of all expression, waiting as the door opened and his presence registered in the next-of-kin's face, Limbe a student of grief, calmly and respectfully delivering the bad news and cataloging the responses to it, a hot shuddering wave passing right through him, a secret burning that only intensified with his efforts to mask it in the face of the plaintive hysterics or mute desolation that the news usually produced.

Each time Limbe knocked on a door, he dismantled a fundamental and cherished illusion: that we own our lives.

He's about to do the same for Mr. Richard Coates.

Limbe walks over and sits down. He sets the attaché case between his feet.

Coates looks over at him and says, "This is highly irregular. I don't appreciate the phone calls. Or the innuendoes either. Why exactly are we meeting here?"

"Patience, Mr. Coates. I'm not here to waste your time." Limbe is momentarily thrown off by the dissimilarity between the brothers, Richard a good five inches taller and lanky, fair-skinned with sharply defined features and fine, straight brown hair. It's only in the stubborn set of his mouth that Limbe sees any connection to Jimmy.

"You haven't told me your name yet," Coates says.

"Not necessary, under the circumstances." Limbe keeps his gaze on the dry fountain, the exposed plumbing in its center, the cracked checkerboard of missing tiles along its sides.

"You're wasting my time," Coates says and starts to get up.

Limbe reaches over and takes Coates by his forearm. "Do you love your wife, Mr. Coates?"

"Why's that your business?"

"You didn't answer my question." Limbe keeps his voice soft and even.

"As a matter of fact, I do. We've been married close to twenty years."

"What would you do for her?" Limbe asks. "Or to keep her in your life for another twenty?"

"This is highly inappropriate," Coates says, "and none of your business."

"Correct on the former," Limbe says, smiling. "And incorrect on the latter."

Limbe picks up the attaché case and sets it on his lap. "Your wife is cheating on you, Mr. Coates."

"That's impossible." Coates's voice breaks a little on the last syllable, and he looks briefly away.

Limbe doesn't say anything. He waits.

He watches Coates debate whether to simply walk off. Coates still believes he owns his life.

Limbe taps the face of the attaché case twice.

Coates clears his throat. "I won't be blackmailed."

"That's not where this is headed, " Limbe says.

"I won't pay you."

Aaron Limbe smiles.

"I should never have agreed to this meeting," Coates says.

"But you did. You were sitting here waiting for me. Why?"

Limbe pauses, then goes on. "I'll tell you. You love your wife. Things have not been quite right between you lately. You don't want to lose her. And if you don't do something, you will. You can't walk away, no matter how badly you want to."

"I've yet to see a shred of proof that what you say is true."

"Are you sure you want that?" Limbe taps the attaché case again.

Coates nods and sits back down on the bench.

Limbe flicks the snaps and takes out a sheath of photographs. He hands them to Coates.

"There's no face," Coates says, after he's riffled through them.

"There's one," Limbe says, "and it's the one that matters. Your wife's."

"I don't understand," Coates says, going through the photographs again, more slowly this time. In each of them, Limbe had cut the head or face of Jimmy Coates out with his Exacto knife.

"Who is he?" Coates asks.

"Natural enough question, " Limbe says, "but not the right one."

Coates looks like he's ready to hit him.

One more push, Limbe thinks.

He snaps the locks on the attaché case and stands up, offering Coates his hand. "They're yours," he says, nodding at the stack of photographs. "No charge." He waits a second before adding that he wishes Coates luck. Even to his own ears, it sounds sincere.

Coates looks up, frowning. "You're giving them to me?"

Limbe nods. "I'm not a blackmailer, Mr. Coates. I already explained that."

Coates sits there, clutching the photos.

Limbe looks at his watch, then adjusts the cuffs of his jacket. "My advice, though, is to forget you ever saw those. Let the affair run its course. Your wife will eventually come back to you. That's the way these things usually work out."

"But," Coates says, then stops. He shuffles through the photographs once more. Limbe knows this time Coates is not seeing the missing face or head and letting his anger bully him. No, this time, he's seeing his wife and what she's doing and how much she's enjoying it.

"You don't understand," Coates says finally. "I love her."

"All the more reason to simply ride this out. You confront her, you force a choice. And it may be one you're not prepared to live with."

"Almost twenty years," Coates says quietly. "I can't stand by and do nothing."

Limbe turns his head and looks through the branches of the trees lining the walk, timing his response. In the distance are the rise and fall of children's voices.

"There are other options," he says.

"What are you suggesting?" Coates has scrolled up the photos so that they resemble a baton in a relay race.

"What you're already thinking," Limbe says.

He sets the attaché case on the ground next to his feet, but remains standing so that Coates has to crane his neck to meet his eyes.

"Let's be blunt, Mr. Coates. You want your wife back. You're also a respected businessman with a reputation to protect. If you're not careful, you're in a position to lose everything."

Limbe points at the rolled-up photos in Coates's fist. "I can make him go away."

"What's that mean exactly?"

"Just what I said."

Coates slowly lets out his breath and begins shaking his head.

"I can make him go away. That's all you need to know," Limbe says. "You don't know my name. You don't know the name of the man in the photographs. You're absolutely in the clear. You simply go on with your life and run your business and wait until you hear from me."

"I can't believe we're having this conversation," Coates says quietly.

"Now you're wasting my time," Limbe says, picking up the attaché case and walking away.

Richard Coates catches up with him at the edge of the plaza. His color isn't good.

"Let's say I agree to your offer," he says and then pauses,

waiting for a group of office workers to pass by on either side of them.

Limbe's anticipated him here, too, figured beforehand that for a businessman like Coates, the asking price had to sting but not draw blood. Whatever his feelings about his wife, Coates would want to know he was getting his money's worth. Limbe thought eight was a little low, twelve a little steep, and had settled on ten.

He steps off the sidewalk and takes out a handkerchief and wipes down the attaché case before setting it between Coates and him.

"Half up front," Limbe says, "by the end of the working day. Same meeting place. Can you swing that?"

Coates nods.

"Good. I'll conclude our business within two days and get back in touch with you. You have the other five ready."

Limbe waits for Coates to pick up the attaché case, and then they walk back toward the courtyard off the old capitol building.

Before they part, Coates has one last spasm of conscience. Limbe smiles and unwraps a breath mint, visualizing Coates's inner turmoil as something like a small piece of meat twitching in a skillet on a burner set too high.

"The time for second thoughts is over," Limbe says. "Do you want to go on with it or not?"

The afternoon sun has burned a little color into Coates's face.

He nods.

TWENTY-TWO

Evelyn's got the Mustang pointed north on Route 17, and she likes the play of the late morning sun on the three thin silver bracelets ringing her wrist and the abrupt music they make each time she shifts gears or changes lanes.

"A whole day," Jimmy says. "How'd you swing it?"

"We have to be back before six." The lie had been easy enough to manufacture, a standard assembly-line version. Richard had committed them to a late dinner engagement that Evelyn knew would eventually double as a business meeting, and she had countered by telling him she was going to get her hair done and buy a new dress.

"It takes a whole day to do that?" Jimmy asks.

"The dinner is important to Richard." She lifts her arm and points past Jimmy, toward the east, in the direction of Squaw Peak and Paradise Valley, home of Josh and Alicia Brandt. Josh was a young hotshot investment counselor who'd relocated from New York, a virtual wizard, according to Richard, at estate planning and restructuring retirement packages. His wife, Alicia, fancied herself an art collector. Evelyn was looking at an evening of anecdotes culled from Josh's weekend adventures as a hot air balloonist and hang-glider and Alicia's nasally outtakes on the local gallery scene. For Evelyn, the evening's prospects had about as much life in them as the tepid minimalist aesthetics that Alicia loved. The evening would be capped by Alicia's condescending surprise and delight that a former airline flight attendant would even know who Agnes Martin or Ad Reinhardt was.

"Something like that," Jimmy says, "You need to bring out the Great Leveler."

"The what?" They've passed the off-ramp for Metrocenter and for the thoroughbred track on Bell Road, and the traffic, like the northern boundaries of the city, is beginning to thin out. Evelyn leans a little harder on the gas.

"You get someone like that Josh or Alicia jamming you up," Jimmy says, "acting like they're better than you, you use the Great Leveler on them. That'll put things into perspective, guaranteed."

The working principle behind the Great Leveler was simplicity itself. All you had to do, Jimmy tells her, is imagine the person getting on your case taking a dump.

"And not some couple-turds-in-the-bowl action or a standard pop-and-drop either," Jimmy says. "For this to work, you have to imagine a monster shit, you know, the kind you really have to work at, feels like your spine's going to snap before you're done, that kind. Doesn't hurt to add some special effects either," he says. "Imagine the person hunched over, hugging his knees, underwear around his ankles, some grimace and squint, and soundtrack the whole thing with a few industrial-strength grunts."

"Stop," Evelyn says, waving her hand. "Just stop, okay?" But it's too late because she's laughing now and because she knows, like the injunction not to think of pink elephants, what will happen when she's sitting across from Josh and Alicia Brandt tonight at dinner.

"Hey, they might not cover it in civics class," Jimmy says, "but if you think about it, the Great Leveler is your basic democracy in action."

"Okay, Jimmy, okay." They've left the city limits behind and have already put the rubble-strewn volcanic beds of Adobe Mountain in the rearview and passed into a stretch of open desert, flat hardpan and the vast blue tumble and reach of sky, a white sun burning its way toward noon.

Evelyn's booked them a room in the Sheraton in downtown Prescott. It's a small, extravagant gesture, impractical and impulsive, that she bent the day to fit. A two-and-a-half-hour drive, three hours in the room, and then the two-and-a-half-hour turnaround.

Within less than ten miles, the landscape begins to change again, open desert giving way to foothills, small clusters and outcroppings of rocks interspersed with saguaro and beavertail cacti, brittlebush and creosote. In the distance is the steady circling of a flock of buzzards, their movements resembling smoke wafting in an updraft of wind.

"Oh man," Jimmy says, thumping the armrest. "I just thought of something. How far are we from a phone?"

"We're just outside New River," Evelyn says. "I need to stop for gas anyway."

"I was supposed to meet Don Ruger today on his lunch break. I forgot all about it until just now."

New River looks anything but new. It's a small, dusty collection of small homes, service stations, family restaurants, and convenience stores.

Evelyn puts in ten dollars of regular. Jimmy makes his call. He comes back out of the store tapping a fresh pack of cigarettes against his wrist and climbs into the car. Evelyn notices, for the first time, he's got on a new white shirt and a new pair of jeans. He's clean-shaven, and his hair has grown out enough that there's something resembling a part running northwest of the stubborn widow's peak.

"Was Don upset?" Evelyn asks. She waits for an opening and then punches back onto 17 North.

"He'll live." Jimmy thumbs the lighter. "He's got this thing he wants me to go in on. The money sounds okay, but the problem is, he got the idea from one of his kids—Gabriella, I think—and she's five years old."

"Does that mean you aren't going to do it?" Evelyn asks.

"I don't know." The lighter pops, and Jimmy pulls it out and jabs at the end of his cigarette. "I don't have all the details yet. And like I said, the money's not bad."

The foothills lengthen. They're at the edge of the Mogollon Rim, about to start a two-thousand-foot ascent. The outcroppings of rock grow larger, more lunar, and eventually loom into jagged mountains and massive rock formations that deepen in color, bands of mauve and orange and pink and ocher. The air starts to thin. The sky tilts.

Evelyn can smell the sunscreen on her bare arms and shoulders. A warm lazy coconut smell.

She's wearing her favorite summer dress, loose and light blue and dotted with small red flowers. She's driving barefoot. It's the heart of the morning.

She feels good and she feels pretty, and right now that's enough, more than enough.

It's been over six weeks since Richard had gone to the convention in Atlanta, and Evelyn has continued to meet Jimmy every chance she gets, but the avalanche of self-recrimination and remorse she's been expecting just hasn't arrived. Evelyn has been looking for signs, the equivalent of loose rocks, the unexpected shifts, that would signal or trigger a slide, but nothing's happened, and she's discovering what the old Evelyn Coates, so tied to duty and the belief she was responsible for everyone's happiness and well-being, never understood: that sometimes there's more ego behind embracing and doing what you believe is expected of you than in pursuing and living out your desires.

She's taken a lover.

She has no excuses. She knows that. But she's not looking for any either. Not anymore.

What she wants instead are the hotel room in Prescott and how they will fill it and the heat and light of this day, the way the sun bakes the flesh and the clear, clean fall of light on the palo verde trees in the washes and on the slopes, the simple surprise of green in the middle of so much rock and desert, and the larger surprise after they reach the summit of the rim and start across the wide plateau that resembles a misplaced piece of the Great Plains, some lost corner of Nebraska or Kansas, herds of Angus and Herefords, a wide, flat blue sky, the grass combed by the wind.

Evelyn looks over at Jimmy and smiles.

"We could just keep going," he says.

"Sure," she says. "I'll drive. You navigate. Where do you want? How about Cleveland? It's nineteen hundred miles. Or Miami, maybe? It clocks in at around twenty-four hundred. New York. It's twenty-five hundred."

"I was thinking Helena," Jimmy says.

"Might as well go to Cleveland," Evelyn says. "At least the Rock and Roll Hall of Fame is there."

Jimmy lights a cigarette and looks away for a moment. "I mean it," he says finally. "We could just skip the hotel, and you could blow off that dinner tonight, and we could just keep going. What's to stop us?"

Evelyn plays along. "Are you saying you want to run off with me?"

He nods. "To Helena."

Evelyn smiles again and changes lanes, passing a dark green minivan loaded with family. "Okay," she says. "I'll run off to Helena with you on one condition."

"What?"

Evelyn says the first thing that comes into her head. "We'll run off, and I'll stay with you until you quit making me laugh or come. Whichever happens first."

"Fair enough," Jimmy says.

He nods one time too many, and Evelyn suddenly realizes it isn't a game, that he's been serious the whole time.

They're fourteen miles outside of Prescott.

Jimmy looks over at her and then digs a penny out of the pocket of his jeans and tosses it on the dash. It catches the sun in a bright coppery flash. He then reaches over and gently touches her right temple with his index finger.

"Okay," Evelyn says, letting out her breath. Her chest is tight. "Is what we have so bad? What's wrong with keeping things like they are?"

Jimmy rubs his cheek. "I need to get out of Phoenix. Too much past and too much looking over the shoulder."

He says something else that Evelyn doesn't catch.

"I said I don't like having to share you either, okay?" Jimmy repeats and looks away.

"Fair enough," Evelyn says quietly.

The road widens to five lanes, and they leave the high-chaparral country and start the final leg to Prescott. The scrub pines disappear, replaced by stands that are thicker and deeper in color and sweep the hillsides, and it's not long before Evelyn can see the sandstone-red lines of the Sheraton sitting atop one of the buttes overlooking the city.

She knows she should be thinking of practicalities and consequences, the price tag on desire, the long reach of her wedding vows, and the life she and Richard have made, a good durable life by anyone's standards, and of the folly of doing anything that would threaten to dismantle it completely.

But she's not.

Instead she's thinking about the moment it all started, her reaching over and pulling down Jimmy's mask in the middle of the robbery of the Tempe branch of Frontier Cleaners, and she's thinking that sometimes folly is all we have, the only thing that matters or that we can truly call our own.

TWENTY-THREE

The Cascade Diner on Van Buren is your basic Crisco Palace, a grease-sheathed throwback to the '50s, a sputtering constellation of neon spelling its name on the sign out front, and inside, cracked leather seats mended with electrical tape, yellowed Formica, slow-motion ceiling fans, heel-worn red-and-white checked linoleum, and large, wide windows slanted like car windshields.

And lots of flies making wing music.

Jimmy and Don Ruger take a window seat. Don had insisted on the Cascade since he's pals with the owner, Walt, who at the conclusion of a meal invariably tells Don his money's no good and makes a show of tearing the tab in half and dropping it in the trash.

Walt's the double-o—owner and operator—of the Cascade and is a short, stocky guy with a black shoe-polish pompadour and a face like an old catcher's mitt and a tattoo with BATAAN AND BACK on his right forearm. He and Don are grayhound fiends and hit the tracks a couple times a week.

Walt comes over to discuss last night's trifecta and lament the legs of Silver Lining in the final stretch and then takes their orders, Don going with the double-cheeseburger combo and Jimmy sticking to coffee and a glass of ice water.

"How much the trifecta set you back?" Jimmy asks after Walt leaves.

"Three hundred and change," Don says. He's got a fresh bandage on the meaty part of his hand at the base of his thumb, a future scar that will join the others, the raised white lines on either hand from running the blades for going on fifteen years at Renzler's Meats.

"You can't ever tell about the legs," Don adds. "When they'll start to go. Silver Lining looked good."

"About tonight," Jimmy says.

Don holds up his index finger and then reaches into his back pocket and pulls out a thin crumpled magazine. He tries smoothening out the pages but finally gives up and slides the thing over to Jimmy.

"You didn't believe me," Don says, "so now you can see for yourself."

Jimmy's about to open the magazine when Walt comes over with their order. He's got a plastic fly swatter attached to one of his belt loops. Jimmy figures you survive the Bataan Death March, you're not going to let a few health code violations get in your way when you're frying burgers.

Or making coffee for that matter. Jimmy had ordered straight black, figuring that was the safest bet, but the cup Walt's poured him has a faint greenish cast even after some vigorous stirring.

Don attacks his double cheeseburger and gives Walt a thumbs-up. Walt, satisfied, nods and heads back to the kitchen. Don pours ketchup next to a mound of fries that look like they've been shellacked.

He picks one up and points with it at the magazine. "Go on and see for yourself," he says and smiles.

It's the same smile Jimmy remembers from the third grade, when he first met Don and they became buddies. The same smile when Don married Teresa, both of them sixteen. The same smile when the kids started, a boy, two girls, and the twins. The same smile when they've had a few rounds at the Chute. The same smile when Don's laid down another of his bets. The same smile when Jimmy had told Don about his plans to run off with Evelyn.

Jimmy looking at the smile, but it's suddenly hard to recognize the rest of the man around it. He's a guy who's saddlebagged at the waist and jowls and wearing a new pair of bifocals. He's a guy with fine streaks of gray in his hair and whose eyes don't quite match the smile anymore.

And Jimmy's suddenly wondering who Don sees when he looks across the table.

Jimmy almost takes a sip of coffee, stops himself, and starts flipping through the magazine.

The figures match, just like Don said.

If the inventory's there, Jimmy's share will be enough scratch to get him to Helena. He doesn't want Evelyn paying his way. That's not how he wants to start things off. Leon's buddy came through with the bartending job. He's expecting Jimmy in a week to ten days.

Jimmy's the one smiling now. Thinking of the job, Evelyn and him in Helena.

His brother can have the farmhouse and the Dobbins parcel. The dry-cleaning chain. The house in Scottsdale. He can have it all. But not Evelyn. She's going with Jimmy.

"Check out page nineteen," Don says. "Brownie the Brown Bear, first generation and hang tags."

What the hell, Jimmy thinks. Knocking over a toy store for a Beanie Baby collection makes as much sense as boosting a Lexus for a chop shop. Same principle. People will put down green for anything.

That's why breaking and entering was invented.

Jimmy figures his teachers, Mom, and Richard had been right all along. There must be something missing in him. He's never wanted things bad enough to work for them. He knows he's supposed to want them, but it never worked out that way. The idea of accumulating a bunch of things just never held any juice for him. That's why it was so easy to take them. Most people had more than they needed anyway, and they always wanted more, and Jimmy basically filled the gap between the attic and the yard sale.

Anything else you had your insurance.

Don finishes his burger and fries and then takes one of his napkins and starts cleaning his glasses.

"What do you think?" he asks Jimmy.

"I'm thinking any time you can ask and get forty-three hundred dollars for Brownie or twenty-four hundred dollars for Humphrey the Camel, you're begging to be taken."

Don nods, smiles, and tells Jimmy that Pete Samoa can fence out the Beanies at top dollar to a collector in San Diego.

"He's also got someone interested in Furbys," Don says.

When Don and Jimmy get to the register, Walt, true to form, takes the tab and rips it in half and tells Don his money's no good. He and Don make plans to hit the track Friday. Walt says he's been hearing some good things about two grays, Aces High and About Time.

Jimmy and Don get in the white Renzler's Meats delivery truck and head for Scottsdale. The place they're going to hit is called The Toy Box and is one of the stores in a small upscale strip mall on Indian School Road.

The strip's anchored by a Mexican restaurant called Manny's, and Don's wife's cousin works there. Don's arranged for him to let them in the rear entrance and into the restaurant's storeroom whose west wall contains the main access to the ductwork for the strip mall's heating and cooling system.

"I was over there earlier in the day," Don says. "The crew came in and ripped out and carted off all the old ductwork. They're going to start installing the new stuff tomorrow."

Don turns his head and winks. "Nothing in that crawl space to get in our way tonight. You cut through the ceiling, drop into the Toy Box, and start filling bags. I got all the tools we need in the back of the truck."

"What's Pete's cut on this?"

"He wanted twenty-five percent, but settled for twenty."

"And Teresa's cousin?"

"Fifty bucks," Don says. "All he's got to do is open a door and walk away."

Don catches a traffic light on the yellow. "You can take out Happy the Hippo, Derby the Horse, Bronty the Brontosaurus, and Bones the Dog from my end when we split. They're the ones I promised I'd get Gabriel and Gabriella."

Jimmy waves that one off and lights a cigarette. He tells Don the Beanies will be his going-away gift to the twins.

"And my going away will be Teresa's present," Jimmy says. It's going on decades of ducking Teresa's wrath whenever he's in the vicinity.

"You never were real good at figuring out Teresa," Don says. "She gets mad when she gets worried, and she only gets worried when she cares about someone." Don thumps the wheel and laughs. "She's been lighting a candle for you, the Wednesday night Mass, going on ten years now."

"You're shitting me," Jimmy says.

"Every Wednesday," Don says. "No lie."

"What's she going to say when you come home with these Beanie things and the cash?"

"She'll go ballistic for a while," Don says, "but the thing is, with Teresa, she'll only ask questions so far, and that's it. The rest she takes to Father Dominguez. She'll cool off in a day or two."

Don slows as they approach the strip mall. It's got a fancy central facade just below the roofline holding the name of the place, East End, and below that the names of the six shops. There's a row of beavertail cacti in a bed of white luckystones along the street and brick planters full of hibiscus fronting the stores. There's a hair salon, a boutique, a computer outlet, a pet accessories shop, then the toy store, and the Mexican restaurant. The restaurant's the only place open.

Don drives around back and parks along the rear wall. There's a small parking lot for employees and one halogen light. Beyond it is an empty lot that eventually runs into the back of a convenience store fronting the next north-south street. Everything's nice and quiet.

Don checks his watch and says Teresa's cousin goes on break in about five minutes. He gets out and unlocks the rear doors of the truck. He's got an extension ladder, an electric saw, two flashlights, some extension cords, and a couple of boxes of jumbo plastic bags stashed there.

Jimmy lights a cigarette and looks around. "What about the noise when we start cutting?"

"Roberto says they got fans going all over the restaurant until the air's fixed. That ought to help cover the worst of the noise. Besides, it shouldn't take long with the saw anyway."

A minute later, just as Jimmy's flicking the cigarette away, the door opens, and Roberto pokes his head out and spots Don. Roberto opens the door wider and disengages the deadbolt. He gives Don a hug. Jimmy figures Roberto for early twenties. He's tall and thin and working mightily on a mustache.

When Don takes out the fifty, Roberto tells him it's not necessary for such a small favor, but Don sticks the bill in the breast pocket of Roberto's white shirt and tells him a young guy can always use some walking-around money.

Don and Jimmy gather the tools, and once they're inside the door, the storeroom's off to their right through another door that's left unlocked until closing. Above the west corner of the storeroom is the open hole that normally would hold a grated ceiling panel. The air-conditioning crew hadn't bothered to replace it. Jimmy sets up the extension ladder and climbs up with the saw and flashlights into the crawl space running the length of the strip mall and then leans over and takes the rest of the stuff Don's carrying.

Don's already red-faced and winded by the time he clears the lip of the hole. He squeezes past Jimmy, and Jimmy reaches down and snags the ladder. It's a tight fit, but he drops the extension, shortening it, and is just able to angle it through the opening.

The crawl space is three and a half feet high, and the flooring is new plywood, which hasn't been nailed down yet. The air's close and hot, and Jimmy's pretty much soaked through his shirt by the time they're above the toy store.

Don locates an outlet along the wall with his flashlight and plugs in the saw.

Jimmy pulls back the plywood, exposing the rafters, then takes the saw and crawls out and begins cutting a long rectangular hole in the three feet of space between each rafter. Within the confines of the crawl space, the saw roars like a plane engine, and Jimmy's breathing sawdust and plaster.

Don slides the ladder between the rafters, and Jimmy again worries the angle, and when he has enough of it through, he opens the extension and pulls up while the lower half falls and then locks into place.

Don tosses over the two boxes of trash bags, and Jimmy tucks the flashlight under his arm and climbs down into the Toy Box.

The front blinds are drawn, so Jimmy fires up the flashlight right away. The toys are laid out on a combination of shelves and tables. Near the cash register is a large aquarium full of small yellow fish with black vertical stripes darting and swarming like sparks from a welding gun.

The collection of retired Beanie Babies are along one wall in a large glass-enclosed case six shelves high. The lock's strictly for show. Jimmy's able to tap it out with a toy hammer. *Beanie Bucks,* Jimmy thinks. It takes five trash bags to empty the shelves. Jimmy carries them over to the ladder and passes them up to Don.

"Don't forget the Furbys," Don whispers.

"What the fuck's a Furby?" Jimmy asks.

"It's just what the name sounds like," Don says, "and they're about four inches tall. Pete said there's been an unexpected run on them at the stores, and he can unload all we can get."

Jimmy hunts down the Furbys and finds a table of them in the center aisle of the store. Under the beam of the flashlight, they look like gigantic hairballs with eyes. They come one to a box, and it takes three more trash bags to get them all. There are four of them out of the boxes on display, and Jimmy tosses those in as well.

It's not long before Jimmy's spooked. He's hearing voices, but what he hears doesn't make any sense. It's just a bunch of shrill jabber, and he's not even sure where it's coming from at first.

"What the hell does 'Doo-moh may-may kah' mean?" he asks when he gets to the ladder. "These things sound like chimps in heat."

Don grabs the first two bags, then the others, and pulls them through the hole in the ceiling.

"I'll be just a second," Jimmy says. He takes a quick look around and figures what the hell, jumping down and making a quick run through the store, loading up a couple trash bags with model dinosaurs, a magic kit, microscope, rocket set, B-B gun, and two baseball gloves.

"Man, what took you?" Don asks. "We need to get out of here."

"Picked up a few things for the other kids," Jimmy says, handing up the bags.

Jimmy drags the ladder back through the crawl space and angles it to the floor of the storeroom.

Roberto's waiting for them. He glances at the pile of plastic bags and then checks his watch, telling Don that it's almost time for the servers to take their last break of the night.

"A bunch of them like to step out back for a cigarette," he says. "It would be a good idea for you to be loaded and gone before they do."

Jimmy carries the tools, and Don two-fists a bunch of the bags holding the Beanie Babies, and they head out the door. Despite the time factor, things are looking good. Don tells Jimmy that Pete Samoa's waiting for them at the Pawn Emporium. Once they drop the stuff off, they can head over to the Chute and catch a few rounds and celebrate.

They toss the stuff in the back of the Renzler's Meats truck and hurry back for another load.

This time Jimmy picks up the bags holding the Furbys. They're still going at it, jabbering away, one voice overlapping the other. He shakes the bags, but that only seems to make it worse, so he speeds it up. Don's a couple of steps ahead of him.

One of the Furbys says, "Dah way-loh" just before the bag explodes.

Don starts to turn and then yells like he's had his hand slammed in a door.

Jimmy's barely had time to register the third shot when Don spins around and crashes into him, knocking Jimmy to the ground and falling on top of him.

There are a couple of more shots. They seem to be coming from the far side of the lot. Jimmy keeps his head low.

Don's moaning, "Man, oh, man," over and over again. Jimmy tells him they've got to get up and move. As in *now.*

Don stops moaning and starts in babbling. He's all over the map. He's talking about Teresa's chile rellenos, Gabriel and Gabriella's first words, a dog named Chip Off the Block that had paid off at six to one, season tickets for the Suns, last month's electric bill, the ceiling fans he still has to hang, and the way the incense at Sunday Mass always makes him sneeze.

Jimmy's plenty scared. He keeps interrupting Don, telling him to get up, but all of Don's weight is on Jimmy, pinning him against the wall.

The shots are coming from across the parking lot, the next north-south street over. Jimmy can hear people shouting.

"Come on, Don," he says.

Jimmy starts pushing against him, trying to lever his way out.

The Furbys are screaming.

Jimmy pushes again.

Don's arm tears free and comes off at the shoulder.

TWENTY-FOUR

It was supposed to have been Jimmy Coates's last night on earth.

That's what Aaron Limbe had intended. Somehow, though, everything had gotten away from him.

He'd killed a cop. And at least two others. There'd been witnesses. He'd shot as many of them as he could, but there'd still be someone who would remember something that would eventually place him. It might take time, but it would happen. Limbe was sure of it. He'd been a cop, after all, for twelve years and knew how witnesses and memory worked. Someone would remember something.

Aaron Limbe checks the rearview and then the speedometer. He's right at the limit. There's a large half-moon to the south, white as a thumbnail under pressure. Limbe is heading for the Mesa View Inn on the slim chance that Coates will double back and grab some of his belongings before he goes to ground.

He checks the rearview again and then unwraps and slips a breath mint onto his tongue.

Tonight was supposed to have been the night. He'd been ready. One clean shot, that's all he needed.

Limbe had staked out the Mesa View Inn shortly after dark and then had followed Coates and Ruger to a diner on Van Buren and later to a strip mall on Indian School Road.

Limbe had taken the next street to the left and pulled into a convenience store lot and parked by a flat, hinged-top, green metal dumpster. Directly below him was a short grassy slope and then southwest, about fifty yards away, was the back of the strip mall. The white delivery truck was about ten yards from the back door to the Mex restaurant. At a diagonal to the truck was a small cluster of cars that Limbe figured to be employee parking. It was a small lot, and the rest of it was empty.

Limbe moved his car a half block up the street and then took the Marlin semiautomatic rifle from his trunk and walked back to the convenience store lot and climbed up on the dumpster and set up shop.

One clean shot.

His eyes had eventually adjusted to the light. One of the halogens behind him, near the street, was on its way out, and it had flickered softly and slowly like a thin stream of clouds passing across the face of the moon.

Limbe practiced sighting on the white delivery truck, then on the back door of the Mex restaurant.

When the back door to the restaurant opened, Limbe had reached over and clicked off the safety on the Marlin. Don Ruger came out first with his hands full of black trash bags, then Coates, who carried an armload of tools.

Aaron Limbe had been ready to pull the trigger when he'd been distracted by movement off to his left, a small flash of red and white that he registered on the periphery of his vision, and by the time he saw it was nothing more than a paper hat caught in a gust of wind, the clerk from the convenience store who'd lost it had spotted him on the dumpster and begun shouting, and Limbe had reflexively swung and fired and taken the kid out.

That momentary loss of concentration hurt, because when Limbe resighted the Marlin, he rushed the shots. Coates and Ruger had been making a second trip to the truck. The first shot hit one of the black plastic bags, the second caught Don Ruger in the shoulder, and the third spun Ruger around and into Coates.

The clerk started dragging himself across the pavement and yelling for help.

A guy at the self-serve pump pointed and shouted something Limbe couldn't catch.

Then there'd been more voices and shouting as people spilled out of the store.

Limbe had expected Coates to break for the restaurant door or the truck, but he'd surprised him by zigzagging across the lot and then rolling across the pavement, taking cover behind the cluster of cars in the employee parking slots.

Limbe laid down a line of fire around and through the cars, keeping Coates pinned, and then ejected the clip and jammed in another.

Everything was starting to get away from him.

The clerk kept calling for help. Limbe shot him again so he wouldn't have to listen to it.

Then he emptied another clip into the cars, hoping to flush Coates out.

While he was reloading, a patrol car pulled into the convenience store lot.

Limbe, at least, had the element of surprise on his side. The police had not been responding to a call. They were on break. They got out of the car and stood in the open while they tried to make sense of what the others were shouting about.

When the guy at the pumps grabbed the first patrolman and pointed in Limbe's direction, Aaron shot him in the stomach, then swung and fired and caught the patrolman in the chest.

He got the second patrolman just as he'd been jumping back into the car.

Limbe emptied the remainder of the clip on the five or six witnesses as they scrambled for the front doors of the convenience store.

As if on cue, there'd been the long, low howl of sirens in the distance.

Limbe reloaded.

He knew Coates would hear those sirens, too.

Coates, though, outwaited him, and Limbe finally had to slide off the dumpster and run the half block north to his car, where he put the rifle in the trunk and then got behind the wheel, counting slowly to ten before he started the car and pulled out in traffic, forcing himself to drive south past the convenience store and slow and gawk like everyone else at the chaos of lights and bodies, and then he made the intersection of Indian School Road and drove west, carefully maintaining the speed limit.

Everything had gotten away from him. Coates was still alive. And Limbe had killed a cop.

He'd seen the second one being helped out of the patrol car when he'd driven past the convenience store, but one dead cop was enough, more than enough, to complicate everything.

Limbe can remember all too clearly the feeling among the rank and file when one of their own went down and the perp was still at large.

He needed to get out of town, but he must do it right, not just run and hope he can stay hidden.

He needs to disappear.

And for that he needs money. Enough money to do it right.

Limbe still has contacts in Nicaragua. They can connect him with people in various parts of Central and South America who have use for his services and talent.

But for that, he needs a stake.

By the time he's made south Scottsdale, Limbe has figured out a way to get it. And the beauty behind the idea is that it will also give him another chance to finish Jimmy Coates.

Limbe scouts out a pay phone and makes two calls, both to the same number.

The first time he talks to Richard Coates and tells him that he's the dispatcher for the Mesa Fire Department and that there's been a fire at his dry-cleaning shop. He assures Coates that it's under control, but adds that it might be a good idea for him to call his insurance company and then come out for a look.

Limbe then walks over to his car and waits five minutes. Then he dials Richard Coates's number again.

Evelyn Coates picks it up on the second ring.

"I'm a friend of Jimmy's," Limbe says, "and he asked me to call you."

"Is he all right?"

"Yes," Limbe says, "considering what happened tonight."

"I was just on my way to meet him," Evelyn says.

"That's why I'm calling. There's been a change in plans."

"He doesn't want to meet at the Plantation Coffee Shop?"

"No," Limbe says. "He's at my place. He thought it would be a good idea to stay off the streets for a while."

"And he's all right?"

"At least for the time being, yes."

There's a pause, then Evelyn says, "I just thought of something. You never told me your name."

"Like I said, I'm a friend of Jimmy's. My name's Aaron. We go back, Jimmy and me. I owe him."

"Can I talk to him?"

"I'm on my car phone, Evelyn. Jimmy asked me to pick you up and take you back to the house. He decided against the coffee shop. Like I said, he figured it'd be better to stay off the streets."

"What's the number at the house?"

Limbe gives it to her. "Jimmy won't pick up though. People have been shot, and he's in trouble, Evelyn. The cops are out looking."

"I don't know," Evelyn says. "I'd feel better talking to him."

"Look," Limbe says. "I'm doing him a favor. If you don't want to see him, we can forget the whole thing. That's okay by me."

"Of course I want to see him."

"Then sit tight, Evelyn." Limbe glances at his watch, then over at his car. "I'll see you in fifteen minutes."

TWENTY-FIVE

Jimmy watches Sammy Jr. of Teater Towing and Auto Service scratch his head and then look up at the office clock. Its hour and minute hands are two crescent wrenches, the numerals lug nuts. Sammy Jr. points out that it's almost 2 A.M.

"I thought the sign said twenty-four hours."

"For towing," Sammy Jr. says. "You need a wrecker, you call and it'll patch into my beeper. You need your car fixed, that's regular hours."

"But you're here now."

"That's true, " Sammy Jr. says.

Jimmy slowly lets out his breath and then asks Sammy if he could fix the brakes on the truck now instead of waiting until morning.

"I might could," he says, "if I had the parts. But that truck of yours is over twenty-five years old."

Jimmy had figured the tranny or radiator would go first, but he'd nursed the pickup through the long steady ascent of the Mogollon on 17 North and had managed to clear the rim. It was the descent that had done him in, the brakes softening and then finally letting go completely by the time he made Cordes Junction, and Jimmy had detoured onto Route 69 and into Mayer, coasting into the service apron of Teater's Auto and then letting his head rest on the steering wheel, his nerves mutinying for the second time that night.

Sammy Jr.'s watching him. Even though he changed before bolting Phoenix, Jimmy reflexively checks his clothes and shoes for blood.

Sammy Jr. palms a can of Dr Pepper and cracks the tab. "I might could put in a call to the original Sammy and see if he could scare you up some brake works." He pauses and sips the soda. "The original Sammy don't sleep any better than me most nights. The family line's full of insomnias."

"I'd really appreciate it." Jimmy wants movement. That's what he needs right now, movement, simple movement, to get his truck back on 17 North to Flagstaff, where he can pick up 40 East and keep going. You can lose yourself in movement, at least for a while. It's stopping or standing still that's unbearable. It feels then as if he's a constant target.

"Insomnia or not," Sammy Jr. says, "it'll cost you extra."

"I figured that," Jimmy says. "How long do you think it'll take?"

"Well, I got to put in the call to my pop, the original Sammy. He lives over at Prescott Valley. Got a salvage yard there. I'll tell him get his flashlight and hunt some brake works. Then I got to drive up there and get them."

Sammy Jr. tells him there's a new Denny's open twenty-four hours across from the Motel 6 about a quarter mile up the road and that Jimmy can wait at either one until the job's done.

"I'd recommend the Six," he says. "You look like you lost a few night's sleep yourself."

Jimmy leaves the service station and sticks to the berm, taking his time. It's a clear night, and the air's thin and chilly. There's a bright half-moon over the old smelter mills in the hills to his left.

All night long he's been alternating between an acid panic and a bone-deep numbness. Nothing at the toy store made any sense, and he still doesn't have all the details, because the radio in the pickup quit working last year and it's too early for the newspapers.

He'd run. He hadn't known what else to do. Don had died, and when the shooting stopped and the ambulances and police cruisers started pouring into the lot of the convenience store, Jimmy had sprinted to the meat truck and quickly driven away. He'd abandoned the truck three blocks from Pete Samoa's Pawn Emporium. He'd been halfway there when he remembered the bags of Beanie Babies and doubled back for them.

Pete, characteristically, claimed the shootings had cut into the market value of the Beanies, making it harder for him to unload them safely, and then had reluctantly agreed afterward to drive Jimmy back to the Mesa View Inn. Jimmy had taken a chance and called Evelyn, lucking out when she answered instead of Richard, and told her he needed to get out of town right away. She agreed to meet him at the Plantation Coffee Shop.

But she hadn't shown up.

Jimmy had waited, sticking around an extra half hour, and then the panics had kicked in again, so he'd left, picking up 17 and heading north.

Jimmy checks into the Motel 6. He's thinking he can call Evelyn in the morning after Richard goes to work and she can drive up and meet him here in Mayer. By that time, too, maybe there will be more news on the shootings.

There's no chance of sleep. Jimmy doesn't want to visit the sideshow his subconscious will work up if he closes his eyes.

So it's the motel room, Jimmy, and the clock. A rerun from his days and nights at Perryville Correctional.

Jimmy waits it out.

The next morning, when he places the call, Jimmy is so used to Richard being Richard and leaving for work with the regularity of someone marching in formation, that he doesn't realize at first that he's just said hello to his brother.

That's the first surprise. The second is that Richard doesn't hang up on him. The third is the panic overriding the customary irritation and impatience in his brother's voice.

"Where in the hell are you, Jimmy? I've been trying to get ahold of you all night."

"Uh, I'm in Mayer." Jimmy takes it slow and careful, but his brother doesn't even bother to ask why.

"Listen," Richard says. "Get back here right away. Come straight to the house. No detours, Jimmy. Do you understand?"

"No," Jimmy says. He doesn't understand.

Then he hears something tear in his brother's voice, and Richard says, "Evelyn. Something's happened to Evelyn."

It's as if Evelyn is in the middle of a crime she can't name. Some immense transgression with no clear boundaries.

She's not even sure Aaron Limbe is his real name.

At first she'd assumed that Limbe had kidnapped her, but when she saw the photos of Jimmy and her thumbtacked to the living room wall, kidnapping didn't make any sense and she started thinking blackmail; but even that dead-ended because if Limbe were going to blackmail anybody, it would have been her, and now she wonders if he's planning to rape her; but even though he's stripped her to bra and panties and tied her to the chair, she can't quite believe rape is where things are heading, or if it is, she doesn't believe it will stop there.

The room is completely dark except for the cone of light from the lamp he's positioned at her left shoulder, adjusting its placement so that the light spills over the wall of photos ten feet in front of her and nowhere else.

She wishes she could wipe away the sweat crawling out of her pores. He's running the furnace on high.

If she could see him, it would be easier to fight back, but he doesn't step into the light. He remains behind her, hovering over her left shoulder, sometimes her right, his movements unpredictable and imperceptible. He's nothing more than a disembodied voice squeezed out of the dark.

He leans in now and asks, "Did you ever pick up a batch of photos, Evelyn, you know, maybe of a special occasion, a family reunion, say, and you start looking through them, and you inevitably come across one or two shots of yourself that throw you off, and you immediately think, 'That's not me. I don't look anything like that'? Hasn't that happened to you?"

Evelyn slowly nods.

"Of course it has," he says. "The image in the photo doesn't match the one you carry around of yourself in your mind, and the easiest solution is to simply throw those unflattering shots of yourself away and forget about them. There are always enough others that fit what you want to see."

Evelyn feels herself begin to tremble.

"Tell me what you see, Evelyn," he says.

She's conscious of the rope binding her ankles to the front legs of the wooden chair and its pull on her wrists behind her.

"Jimmy and me," she says quietly.

"True," he says. "And what are you doing?"

"I don't know what you want me to say."

"Just tell me what you see."

"We're making love," she says.

Evelyn hears him slowly let out his breath. "No," he says. "You're wrong, and you're afraid, Evelyn, but it's not the kind of fear that will take us where we need to go."

A moment later, he leans over and pulls her hair away from her face and then stretches a wide swath of silver duct tape across her mouth.

It's leaning on noon, and his brother's been drinking. From where he's sitting, Jimmy can't tell how much of a dent Richard's made in the bottle of Wild Turkey, but from the look of him, Richard must have been up all night, too.

They're in the small office Richard maintains in the house at Scottsdale on the second floor, down the hall from the master bedroom. There's a stripped-down military feel to the room, all right angles and neutral colors.

Jimmy's trying to process what his brother's just told him.

The words are still playing in Jimmy's head, Richard's maddeningly precise account of how he hired someone to kill his wife's lover.

And then Richard giving him the details of act 2 when the whole thing backfired and the hired killer turned kidnapper and snatched Evelyn.

He wonders if his brother has drunk enough whiskey to find the courage to shoot him.

Because Jimmy figures that's what he's walked into. They're in tabloid territory now, the finale to some third-rate tragedy destined to be supermarket-aisle headlines.

Richard picks up the bottle, hesitates, and then sets it down.

Jimmy watches his brother's hands and eyes.

"He said it had to be you," Richard says finally. "You had to be the one to deliver the money. No one else. Those were his conditions."

Jimmy's suddenly having trouble reading the compass.

"That's why I needed you back here. He'll only deal with you."

"I don't get it," Jimmy says.

"He's the type of people you associate with," Richard says. "I just didn't see it at the time."

In a blink, he and Richard are back on familiar ground.

Maybe, but I've never hired out someone hit, Jimmy thinks.

To Richard, he says, "There's a lot of things you don't see, basically because you're so busy being right all the time."

"You'd never understand," Richard says, waving him off. "You can't. You've never loved anyone."

Richard leans back in his chair, closing his eyes and bridging his temples with his thumb and index finger. "We're talking about Evelyn," he says quietly. "Almost twenty years. You'll never be able to understand a love like that. If I'd known who it was, I'd have gone after him myself."

"What are you talking about?"

"This." Richard picks up a manila envelope from the desk and throws it at Jimmy.

Jimmy flips through a stack of black-and-white photos of Evelyn and him. In each, his head or face has been cut out.

"I had to," Richard says.

Jimmy slips the photos back in the envelope. He thinks about being pinned down in the parking lot of the strip mall. About Don Ruger's arm coming off at the shoulder.

"He never told you his name?" Jimmy asks.

Richard says no.

"What'd he look like then?"

Richard goes back to massaging his temples. "I don't know. He was average looking. Medium build. Short black hair. He kept popping breath mints the whole time we talked. And he had these pale gray eyes, they made you nervous when he looked at you. That's all I can remember."

That was enough though.

"How much is the ransom?" Jimmy asks.

Richard sits back in his chair. He looks at the bottle of Wild Turkey. "Fifty grand. By the close of working hours today."

"And you can get ahold of that kind of money?"

"If I have to," Richard says. "I made a couple of calls and put a lien on the Dobbins parcel. The bank will come through with the money. All you have to do is deliver it."

Sure, Jimmy thinks. *That's all. And give Aaron Limbe another chance to finish the job you hired him to do.*

The muscles in her legs and back have begun to cramp. The floor vents are pouring heat. The room is dark except for the spill of light on the wall of photographs.

Aaron Limbe drops his hand on the back of Evelyn's neck.

"I'm thirsty," she says.

"Of course you are, Evelyn. Now tell me what you see."

"Tell me what you want to hear," she says, "and I'll say it. Whatever it is, just tell me." She closes her eyes for a moment.

"You're missing the point. This is not about what I want to hear."

"Why are you doing this?" Evelyn's throat is parched, her voice scratchy. "You told me you were a friend of Jimmy's."

"Jimmy Coates is a mongrel," Limbe says, "as worthless as any nigger or taco-bender, and I have numbered his hours."

He puts one hand at the base of her skull and the other along her jawline and locks his fingers into place. Evelyn can't move her head. He moves it for her.

"One at a time," he says, levering and directing her line of vision. "Starting at the top left. And don't close your eyes, Evelyn. If you do, we'll have to start all over again."

He guides her picture by picture, lingering on each, one row after another, seventy-two photos in all.

"You're still fighting me, Evelyn," he says when they're done. "I could feel the tension in your neck, the resistance the whole time. You still refuse to see." For a moment, he sounds genuinely sorry.

Then he brings out the duct tape again.

His hand is back on her neck, hard.

"Look at the wall, Evelyn. That's not making love. We're not talking about love. It's friction. Fucking. Fornication. It's two animals in heat."

When she tries to shake her head, his fingers lock on the tendons cording her neck. Small patches of white and yellow swim into her peripheral vision.

"Look at yourself in those photos, Evelyn. What you're doing. Look at the way you spread your legs. Look at what you're doing with your hands, your mouth. Look at what you let be done to you."

No, she thinks. *No. This isn't happening.*

"Jimmy Coates ruins everything he touches, and you let him between your legs and took him inside you. He ruined you, Evelyn. You're a fallen woman. That's what people used to call someone like you when I was a child. Fallen." He pauses, and she feels his breath as well as his fingers on her neck. "You'll understand what Jimmy Coates is once you accept what you've become."

No.

It's the only word that makes sense, the one she repeats to herself while Aaron Limbe continues to talk, *No,* over and over, to the way he's twisted things, because she knows who she is and what Jimmy and she had together, knows how passion can burn you clean of everything except itself and how there is a grace in the trembling of flesh before flesh and how in the moment of its joining you simultaneously find and lose yourself, and that's all love has ever been or will be, the finding and losing of yourself in the touch of another, and that's enough, more than enough, and probably more than any of us deserve, and if she could, if it weren't for the duct tape stretched tightly across her mouth, she'd scream the NO she's been repeating to herself in Aaron Limbe's face, a NO as stubborn, resolute, and defiant as she could make it, but right now she's afraid because she's having difficulty remembering what Aaron Limbe looks like, and she needs to remember that, to hold on to his image, because it's easier to fight back then, but Aaron Limbe has slowly turned into his voice, and like the darkness it arises from, the voice swallows all contexts except its own, and Evelyn's afraid to close her eyes because that would be like inviting the voice and the darkness in, but what light she's left with only leads to the wall and the photos covering it, and because of that, everything has shrunken to the NO she's holding deep in her chest like a breath.

By 3 P.M., a pot of coffee has sobered Richard up, and he's showered, shaved, and changed suits and gone on to pick up the ransom money at the bank.

Jimmy's sitting behind the desk in the second-floor office. He picks up the phone and punches out Pete Samoa's number.

"Oh man," Pete says after a moment. "This sounds like a local connection. Please tell me I'm wrong here."

"Have the cops been around?"

"Of course. You left the Renzler's truck three blocks away. What did you think? They're all over the place on this one. A cop got killed. They're not going to leave it alone any time soon. I was able to tell them you were out of town, keep everything nice and neat. And then what? You show up again."

"Look, Pete, I need to talk to Ray Harp."

"You're out of town and clear. Then you come back. I'm still not believing this."

"It's important. I need to get ahold of Ray."

"He won't talk to you. Not now." Pete goes on about Ray Harp's troubles with Limon Perez and the Mexican gangs and Newt Deems getting shot and ending up in intensive care.

"It's Limbe," Jimmy says. "I need to talk to Ray about Limbe."

Pete doesn't say anything for a moment.

"Come on," Jimmy says. "Give me the number."

"It won't do you any good. Aaron Limbe is AWOL. He doesn't work for Ray anymore. He walked about four days ago, right around the time all the trouble started with Perez. That's all I can tell you. No one's seen him around."

That's it, Jimmy thinks, feeling his hope evaporate. Ray Harp was his best chance at curbing Aaron Limbe. Jimmy figured he'd offer Ray a cut from the ransom if he'd step in. Limbe was used to taking orders from Ray, and with the right leverage, Ray might have just been able to get Evelyn back unharmed. It was a bread-and-butter plan, a basic end run, the only thing Jimmy could come up with that might work.

Jimmy racks the phone and then looks down at his hands. After a while, he gets up from the desk and wanders down the hall. He stands in the doorway of the master bedroom, looking in, listening to the sound of his breath, until he hears Richard return.

The money is in a tan canvas bag. A pair of cuffs dangles from its grip. Jimmy sits down at the kitchen table across from his brother, and they wait for the phone and more instructions from Aaron Limbe.

Behind and to her left, Aaron Limbe talks about the true world and the ascendancy of form revealed in the universal hierarchy and about the nature and breadth of consequence leading to the works of a true and perfect wrath.

"There's no room for forgiveness," Limbe tells her. "There never has been. Jesus wanted to be loved. So he lied. A failed romance, that's all the New Testament is. A second-rate love story."

He steps over and places his hand on Evelyn's head, his fingers lightly resting in her hair.

A thing is what it's named, he tells her.

Whore, for example.

Adulterer.

Cunt.

Then his foot abruptly snakes around the leg of the chair and pulls it off center and out, slamming her to the floor. Evelyn lies on her side, sweat sheeting her, trying to take in enough air to keep from blacking out.

Limbe rights the chair with her still in it, waits a few seconds, and then kicks the leg out again. Her right shoulder takes the brunt of the fall this time.

She won't cry. She won't give him that.

She's not sure how many times he repeats the sequence. She can't anticipate how long he'll wait before he steps in again and kicks the chair out and lets gravity claim her. Her right shoulder burns, and her spine aches. Her breath is three steps ahead of her.

When she looks at the wall of photos this time, it seems impossible that the body she inhabits in them had ever felt pleasure or joy or desire, in fact, felt anything beyond thirst, pain, and exhaustion. What she sees, over and over again in the rows, is flesh and its demands.

Limbe twists the neck of the lamp, adjusting the fall of light, the black-and-white photos disappearing and Evelyn's chest, lap, and legs jumping into stark relief.

Limbe unties the ropes binding her wrists. Her hands are numb. He takes them and sets them in her lap.

He then peels away the duct tape, giving her voice back to her, but her words, like the feeling in her hands, have fled, and Evelyn's afraid to open her mouth and do anything but breathe. She's seized by nightmare logic, afraid that if she tries to speak, nothing at all will happen or that it will be Limbe's voice and words that spill from her mouth.

Limbe drops a manila envelope in her lap and tells her to open it.

Evelyn can't make her fingers move.

Limbe says something about a Laundromat, Jimmy owing money.

"Look at the envelope, Evelyn. Who it's addressed to. Then look at the handwriting."

He waits a moment, then says, "I took the envelope from your lover. He doesn't know I have it. He was going to send it to your house, Evelyn. To your husband."

Limbe reaches down and squeezes her right hand hard. "Open it."

She bends her head and slowly works her nails under the flap of the envelope and tears it open.

She slips her hand inside. *No,* she thinks. *No.*

"Meat," Aaron Limbe says. "That's all you are and ever have been to Jimmy Coates. Nothing more than a way of getting back at his brother."

No, she thinks.

"Tell me about love, Evelyn," Aaron Limbe says.

She closes her eyes.

The manila envelope falls to the floor.

Montana was supposed to have been a blank page for both of them, she thinks.

She's left holding a wadded pair of blue panties.

Evelyn remembers standing amidst the chaos of Jimmy's room at the Mesa View Inn and lifting one leg, then the other, as Jimmy peeled them off, then later that night, looking for them as she dressed to go home.

And then she's crying.

Despite everything she's told herself, Evelyn's crying, great chest-wrenching sobs that run into each other like waves and come from some place far off that she now can barely remember.

She holds the panties tight in her fist and cries. She can't stop. She doesn't even try to.

Aaron Limbe adjusts the lamp again. The north wall of the living room and the photos swim back into focus and hold.

Evelyn bows her head. She's still clutching the panties.

After a moment, Aaron Limbe reaches over and lifts her chin.

"Tell me what you see, Evelyn," he says. "Then you can get

dressed, and we'll take a little ride to West Dobbins for the big reunion."

"He wouldn't let me talk to her," Richard says. "He wanted to make sure I had the money. I don't even know if Evelyn's alive. It's going on nineteen hours."

Jimmy looks at the canvas bag sitting on the kitchen table. His brother crosses the room and draws a glass of water. "He said you're supposed to go someplace called the Chute at five, and he'd call you there with the final instructions."

"Keep it on his terms," Jimmy says. He can hear the subtext creeping into Richard's voice. "No cops."

"But they know how to handle things like this. They're professionals. He's given us an opening, mentioning the Chute." Richard sets the glass down on the counter. Behind him, the bay window opens onto the afternoon sky. It's filled with sour yellow light, different from the usual late-summer haze of thermal inversions, and reminds Jimmy of a piece of old newspaper.

"He's testing you," Jimmy says finally.

"Why should I believe you?"

"Because I know who we're dealing with. You don't want to do something like that, believe me, with this guy."

There's a long pause, and then Richard says, "I don't like the idea of Evelyn's life being in your hands."

"It's not. It's in yours, Richard. And if you bring in the cops, her blood will be on them. I guarantee it."

There's another long pause, and Jimmy can sense Richard's about to go self-righteous on him and decides he'd better shut him down quick.

"You're forgetting something else, Richard. You hired the guy to kill someone. You really think it's a good idea to get the cops involved? You ready to face what might shake out if they catch the guy?"

Richard checks his watch. "I'm going with you then."

"No way," Jimmy says.

"I have to go. I can't count on you to follow instructions."

Richard points at the canvas bag. "That's a lot of money, and it's the only thing that's going to get Evelyn back."

Jimmy lets out his breath. "You're not in charge here, Richard. You keep forgetting that. You can't change the conditions for delivering the ransom at the last minute."

"Why you?" Richard asks. "Anybody but you."

He turns briefly away, then turns and steps in and hits Jimmy. It's a straight sucker punch. Jimmy's head snaps back. A second later, he's tasting blood.

Richard hits him again, catching him on the side of the face. Jimmy's flailing his arms and trying to set up, but Richard has the reach, those long arms of his, and catches him again, and this time Jimmy's on the floor.

Richard stands over him, opening and closing his fists like gills.

Jimmy slowly gets up and heads for the sink and splashes some cold water on his face. Drying up, he notices a pair of steel barbecue tongs in the dish rack. He looks over his shoulder at Richard, then slips the tongs in the back pocket of his jeans and pulls his T-shirt over them. He walks back over to the kitchen table and picks up the canvas bag.

"I need to be going," Jimmy says.

"Anybody but you," Richard says again, but lets him past.

On the way to the Chute, Jimmy conjures up Evelyn. They're on their way to Montana. She's sitting next to him, her feet up on the dash, and at a glance, Jimmy can take in the small bright splashes of red nail polish and the long lines of her legs, the inverted *V* they make.

The reverie, though, quickly sputters out.

Jimmy tells himself he has to stay focused on what needs to be done, but the self-doubts and panics keep crowding him. At best, he has a couple of ideas that, taken together, don't quite add up to a plan. Aaron Limbe's holding the patent on everything else.

At the Chute, Jimmy takes a stool at the end of the bar near the pay phone. He's got the canvas bag handcuffed to his left wrist. Leon Glade is tending. Jimmy looks around, then reaches into his back pocket for the stainless steel barbecue tongs.

"Hey, Leon," Jimmy says, clicking them twice. "I need to talk to you for a minute."

TWENTY-SIX

Aaron Limbe set the meet at Jimmy's grandfather's place, the old farmhouse on West Dobbins. Jimmy's parked his pickup a hundred yards from the entrance to the driveway, figuring that given the condition of the truck's exhaust system, anything closer would have been the equivalent of hiring a marching band to announce his arrival.

The wind has picked up, and the sky is the color of butter gone bad. The signs have been following him around all afternoon, and Jimmy's been tracking the progress of the storm in his rearview, a half-mile-high wall of dust, all swarm and roil, sweeping in from the east and spreading across the entire Maricopa Valley. He figures he has fifteen, maybe twenty, minutes before it catches up with him.

The gate at the end of the drive is closed but not locked. The house sits about a quarter of a mile in on a flat rise, the four-acre stretch that had once been the front yard now completely feral, dense with vegetation and thicket-ridden, strewn with scattered outcroppings of rock and junk the locals have dumped over the years.

Near the top of the drive, Jimmy locks the cuffs on the canvas bag to his left wrist and takes out a Smith & Wesson 3904 from the waistband of his jeans. The gun's a Pete Samoa special, a third- or fourth-generation pawn, the serial number filed down, the grip secured with electrical tape, a nine-millimeter auto that's basically a collection of lethal scrap masquerading as a firearm, but it's the only thing Jimmy could come up with on short notice.

He leaves the drive, ducks through a tangle of mesquite and creosote and tarbush and works his way toward the front of the house. The wind kicks in stronger, leaves and branches rattling and chattering with each sustained gust, the air darkening.

He needs to make sure Evelyn's in the house. Jimmy's under no illusion that this is a standard-issue kidnapping. No way he can walk in with the cash and walk out with Evelyn. Not with Aaron Limbe calling the shots.

Jimmy edges along the east wall of the house. Limbe's car is parked out back on the wide gravel apron fronting the orchard and storage shed. From what Jimmy can tell, the front of the house is empty.

The air's turned grainy, and the wind hisses like the rush of a faucet opened wide.

He seals off the part of his brain setting odds that Aaron Limbe has already disposed of Evelyn's body.

He keeps checking windows.

He finds her in the dining room off the kitchen. She's tied to a chair in the middle of the floor. All the furniture has been moved and pushed off to the side. In the corner are a large toolbox and a pile of power tools. Evelyn's staring straight ahead, toward the front of the house. There's no sign of Limbe.

Jimmy remains crouched at the bottom edge of the window and reins in the urge to tap on the glass. The dust is blotting out the afternoon. The wind driving it feels like someone's jabbing him hard in the back of the neck with the stiff end of a broom.

Evelyn doesn't glance his way once.

Jimmy finally breaks from his crouch and sprints to Aaron Limbe's car. It's unlocked. He slips inside and hot-wires it. Once the idle has smoothed, he reaches up and puts the car in gear and lets it roll slowly down the gravel apron toward the driveway. Jimmy jogs along with it, keeping the car between the house and him.

Come on, he thinks. *Come on.*

He leans through the driver's window and taps the horn twice.

A few seconds later, the kitchen door opens.

Jimmy raises the Smith & Wesson.

The world disappears in a gust of wind.

Everything's reduced to a muddy-brown churn and choke. It's as if he's trapped inside an immense vacuum cleaner.

The car stalls out.

Something moves off to his right.

Jimmy fires. He wants to end it and end it now, to footnote Aaron Limbe and take him right off the page.

The back windshield of the car explodes.

The earth and sky tear themselves apart.

Jimmy fires again. He keeps his finger on the trigger and swings his arm, trying to space and place his shots. Limbe's ghosting every one. Tracking him through the storm is like trying to step on your own shadow.

"That's eight," Limbe calls out.

Jimmy drops next to the left front tire. He kicks out the magazine on the 3904 and starts scrambling through his pockets for reloads. He's got dirt in his eyes, and he's fighting the urge to rub them, knowing that will only make it worse, but his vision's the equivalent of a mud-streaked windshield. There's no teamwork among his fingers either. He's dropping bullets everywhere.

He suddenly thinks of his buddy, Don Ruger, dying in the parking lot of a toy store.

Jimmy's started talking to himself, anything to slow that long slide into pure panic where there's nothing but nerve endings and no excuses or help.

Right now, he's floating hope like a loan.

He manages to thumb two bullets into the magazine.

When he looks up, Aaron Limbe is standing next to him.

TWENTY-SEVEN

With all the furniture pushed aside, the house has an off-balance, lopsided feel to it, as if Jimmy were stuck inside a ship that had run seriously aground.

Evelyn's still in the chair. Aaron Limbe is standing behind her. He's holding Jimmy's Smith & Wesson auto in his right hand.

Jimmy barely recognizes Evelyn. Her face is drawn, battered from lack of sleep, and her eyes are raccooned, her posture crushed. The rumpled white T-shirt and jeans hang on her frame. Everything about her looks punished and diminished.

Limbe places his hand on top of Evelyn's head. "We're going to finish this now, Evelyn," he says softly. "It's time. You understand that, don't you, even if Jimmy doesn't."

Limbe drops his hand to the back of her neck. "Where we are now," he says, "is what happens any time Jimmy Coates steps into someone's life."

"Evelyn," Jimmy says, but she won't look at him. Her shoulders start to shake, and she lowers her head.

"You never know if love's true unless it's tested," Limbe says.

He tosses the Smith & Wesson over to Jimmy.

After catching it, Jimmy kicks out the magazine. It's empty.

When he looks up, Limbe's holding a nine-millimeter bullet between his thumb and index finger.

"One shot," Limbe says. "I'm giving you a chance to save her."

He walks over and sets the bullet on the counter separating the dining room and kitchen.

"Come on," Limbe says. "You love her, don't you, Jimmy?"

Jimmy takes a couple of steps, hesitates, then stops. He looks around the room and then back at Aaron Limbe. The bullet's ten feet away. "I don't get it," he says.

Limbe pulls a .38 from the small of his back and waves his arm, pointing the gun in Evelyn's direction, then Jimmy's. "You'll do it if you love her."

"What?"

"Kill her," Limbe says.

"You can't be serious." Jimmy hears his voice breaking. "That doesn't make any sense."

"Sense is not something you make," Limbe says. "It's something revealed to those who have prepared themselves."

He's got hands like a kid, Jimmy thinks. He's not sure why he's just gotten around to noticing that. With Aaron Limbe, it had always been the eyes that snagged you first, that pale gray dead-end stare that unnerved and spooked you, the rest of Limbe taking a backseat to those eyes, leaving him with the generic bearing of a mortician during calling hours, a presence you registered but never quite fully took in.

"You're both going to die," Limbe says. "That's not the point. The point is who goes first." He pauses, then adds, "A chance to save her is what I'm offering you."

"I still don't get it," Jimmy says. "I'm supposed to kill Evelyn to save her? From what, exactly?"

"From what I'll do to her if I end up having to kill you first."

Limbe's smiling now, waiting for Jimmy to work out the exact dimensions of what they're looking at.

"No way," Jimmy says finally. "No way I'm going to do something like that."

Limbe turns and picks up an electric belt sander from the pile of tools in the corner, then walks over to Evelyn and rests the sander along the inside of her upper left thigh.

"Think about it," he says.

Despite himself, Jimmy does. He can't help it. His gaze keeps traveling from the sander and then down the length of Evelyn's thigh to the knee of her jeans and back again, Jimmy not able to do anything but think about that wide black tongue of sandpaper and Limbe's finger on the switch.

Limbe tosses the sander back on the floor. "What's it going to be, Jimmy? Do you love Evelyn enough to kill her or not?"

Evelyn lifts her head and looks at Jimmy for the first time. She mouths the word *Please.*

"That's all you need," Limbe says. "Love and one correctly placed shot." He reaches over and touches the base of Evelyn's neck.

Evelyn won't break eye contact now. She's looking straight at Jimmy. It's the same look she'd given him on those nights when she'd stood in his room at the Mesa View Inn and started to undress.

Jimmy walks over to the kitchen counter. Aaron Limbe follows, standing behind him as Jimmy picks up the bullet and thumbs it into the magazine of the Smith & Wesson and they walk back into the middle of the dining room.

Here we go, Jimmy thinks, lifting the pistol.

He places the Smith & Wesson against his right temple.

"Wait a minute," Limbe says. "What are you doing?"

Jimmy hefts and shakes the canvas bag handcuffed to his wrist. "You screwed up, Aaron," he says. "How do you know the money's all here? What if I stashed it somewhere else?"

Limbe doesn't say anything.

"It's your turn to think about it," Jimmy says. "Fifty thousand bucks. What if it's not here, and I shoot myself? What are you going to do then?"

"You fucker," Limbe says quietly.

"Let her go," Jimmy says, "and we deal."

"No," Limbe says. "That's not acceptable. She stays. She can ID me. We finish it."

"How far are you going to get on what's in your pockets, Limbe? You killed four people, one of them a cop."

Limbe shakes his head. "Where we are is nonnegotiable, Coates. I said no."

For a while, the only sound is that of wind pushing dust and the creak of rafters.

Jimmy keeps the Smith & Wesson 3904 wedged against his temple. Limbe has the .38 pointed at Jimmy's chest. They wait each other out.

A little Hollywood Logic, Jimmy thinks.

That's what he's counting on, some Hollywood Logic, what Howard Modine, his philosophy prof drinking buddy, used to rail about at the Chute over some cold ones, Modine going on and on about how the Citizens based their lives on Hollywood Logic, an unswerving belief that the Big Script, no matter how bad things looked, always held the ending they wanted.

Howard Modine, though, never had to stare down Aaron Limbe. Sometimes Hollywood Logic was all you had.

Jimmy decides it's time to ride it out.

He glances over at Evelyn, giving Limbe the opening he's been waiting for and trying not to be obvious and italicize it.

Limbe quickly drops his arm, feints to the left, then abruptly cuts right and knocks Jimmy off his feet. Limbe grabs the Smith & Wesson and tosses it against the wall. He pins Jimmy to the floor, one knee on his chest, the other on the bicep of his left arm. He puts the .38 in Jimmy's face and with his left hand pulls over the canvas bag handcuffed to Jimmy's wrist.

On the periphery of his vision, Jimmy sees Evelyn slowly lower her head.

Limbe keeps the gun and his gaze trained on Jimmy while he reaches over and unzips the bag. Jimmy begins to deejay it, slipping into a soft, fast patter, hoping the words he's running will be enough of a distraction.

Limbe works his hand inside the bag and smiles.

"Nice try, Coates." He pulls out a stack of bound bills and drops them on the floor, then reaches inside the bag again, riffling deeper this time.

And then it happens.

Jimmy can read it in Limbe's face even before he yells out.

Limbe jerks his hand free of the bag. The sidewinder from the Chute comes with it. The snake's a foot and a half of writhe and venom and has its fangs embedded in the underside of Limbe's wrist.

Limbe's yelling and trying to shake the sidewinder off and shoot Jimmy at the same time.

He rocks back, his center of gravity shifting, and Jimmy's able to throw him off balance and grab the arm with the gun. He brings it down upon the floor hard, then scrambles for the .38.

He hears the sidewinder's rattles going somewhere above his head.

Jimmy begins hitting Limbe with the pistol and keeps hitting him until Limbe rolls off and onto the floor.

Jimmy's on his feet fast. "Where is it?" he asks Evelyn. "Where'd it go? The snake?"

"Over there," she says, nodding in the direction of the wall with a section of floor molding missing. "I think it crawled under the house."

Aaron Limbe's rolling slowly around on the floor and mumbling some hybrid threat and curse. He keeps lifting his left arm and throwing it at his right leg.

Jimmy unties Evelyn. She picks up the .38 and hands it back to Jimmy.

"Finish it," she says.

She turns and crosses the room, stopping at the kitchen counter, where she takes a large manila envelope and checks its contents, then walks back over to Jimmy and tells him she needs to borrow his lighter. After that, she heads for the kitchen door and outside.

Jimmy's circling the dining room and Aaron Limbe. He keeps glancing down at the gun in his hand and then over at the missing piece of molding at the base of the west wall. He's got the sweats.

"Finishing it" has never been one of his strong suites.

Limbe's trying to sit up. His eyelids are fluttering. There's a pocket of whitish drool gathered at the corner of his mouth.

Jimmy steps up and points the .38 at the back of Limbe's head. One small electrical impulse, he tells himself, one zap to the right set of nerve endings, a flashpoint, and then his finger will move and finish it for him. Simple. Nothing more elaborate than snagging and pulling the pop-top back on a can of beer.

Except Jimmy can't do it. As badly as he wants to, as much as he knows he needs to, he can't pull the trigger on Aaron Limbe. It just isn't in him.

Limbe's having trouble sitting up and maintaining his balance. He keeps throwing his left arm toward his ankle. He's mumbling something Jimmy can't catch.

Jimmy tucks the pistol into his pants and moves fast, not wanting to think too long about what he's going to do. He unlocks and removes the handcuffs from the canvas bag, then turns and knocks Limbe back to the floor, grabs him under the arms, and drags him into the kitchen.

Limbe fights him, but Jimmy eventually gets one end of the cuffs around Limbe's right wrist and the other around the knob of the pantry door and snapped closed.

Jimmy steps back. Limbe pulls against the cuffs, setting off a long rattle. "You'll see," he says between breaths.

"What, see?" Jimmy asks.

Limbe keeps rattling the cuffs. His face is blotchy and damp. "You'll see," he says again.

Jimmy heads for the kitchen door.

Outside, every trace of the dust storm has vanished. The wind is gone, and the light has a sharp, brittle edge. The sky has reopened, immense and bright and depthless, and is much too blue, the shade that Arizona always peddles to tourists.

Evelyn is behind the house, crouched at the edge of the gravel driveway apron. She has a small fire going and a stack of photographs piled at her feet. She feeds them one at a time to the flames. She doesn't look up when Jimmy walks over.

"Is he dead?" she asks.

"He's on his way," Jimmy says and tells her about the cuffs.

Evelyn slips another black-and-white photo into the flames.

The Mesa View Inn. Evelyn crouched in front of Jimmy in her panties and unzipping his jeans. Evelyn with a Mona Lisa smile. Jimmy with his hand in her hair.

"He cut out my face," Jimmy says, "on the ones he sent to Richard."

Evelyn nods and picks up the next black-and-white from the pile.

Jimmy waits, hoping Evelyn will add something or at least look at him instead of the photos, but she's in lockdown mode, there and somewhere else at the same time, no different from the planes still stranded and stacked in all that blue above them to the north circling and waiting for clearance from the tower at Sky Harbor International.

Jimmy walks a little farther into the backyard. To his right is a dilapidated wooden storage shed and behind that the remains of the orchard, the oranges and lemons hanging from branches like forgotten Christmas ornaments.

Luck, he tells himself. All they had to do is ride the luck. It's breaking their way, and when it does, you don't question it. You ride it all the way out.

In a little while, he'll scare up a shovel from the shed and bury Limbe behind the orchard. Then Jimmy will take Limbe's car and put it out back with the rest of the junk and torch it. He'll talk to Evelyn afterward, work on getting their stories straight. Jimmy's got some plans for the ransom money, and there's no reason to let his brother, Richard, in on them.

No, Jimmy's going to play it as if everything went Limbe's way. Let Richard believe he followed instructions and got Evelyn back unharmed. No snake. No secret grave. No torched cars. Straight business.

Everything's going to work out just fine, Jimmy's sure of it now, Evelyn and him walking away, clear and clean, outside of anything the cops or Richard can do about it or them.

When Jimmy turns around, Evelyn is standing in front of the fire, the pile of photographs gone. She rummages in the front pocket of her jeans, pulls out something small and soft blue that's wadded like a piece of paper, and looks briefly over at him before dropping it in the flames. Then she turns and starts toward the house.

"What are you doing?" Jimmy asks when he catches up with her.

"I want to watch."

"Oh man, give it a little more time, Evelyn. A snakebite, what it does, believe me, that's not something you want to see."

"That's where you're wrong, Jimmy," she says. "More wrong than you'll ever know."

She brushes by him, and then she's through the door and in the house, and Jimmy, shaking his head, walks over to the shed to look for a shovel.

TWENTY-EIGHT

Aaron Limbe knows this: what it means to burn.

There is blood, and there is burning, and there is the heart that pumps them both, and that's where he lives, where he's always lived, in the burning and with the burning, and he's witnessed its power and true form, and at times been its instrument and agent, and he's come to understand there's a burning that in itself does not burn, that when loosed upon the world consumes all that is not itself, a burning that burns away the accidental and incidental and the fortuitous, that clarifies and therefore purifies all which is false and not of itself, because that which is false is without purpose, and to be without purpose is to be without form, and that without form is weak and broken and lost and does not last, but he who lives within such burning will come to learn all the secrets of the blood and the form the heart bestows upon them, and he is then with purpose and therefore emptied of everything not of himself and lives in the knowledge that what is left is forever who you are and that who you are is forever burning.

He is waiting for the door to open again.

When it finally does, Aaron Limbe pulls himself from the floor to a sitting position. The skin on his face is hot and tight and puffy, and his eyes have almost swollen shut.

Aaron Limbe looks down at his left hand and slowly moves its fingers.

He coughs, and the cuffs bite into his right wrist. His head drops back against the pantry door. There's a tightness in his temples and an avalanche of a headache breaking loose in his skull. Every other breath is shadowed by a wheeze. Something leaks from the corner of his mouth down his chin.

There's something he's supposed to be remembering. It's important.

His arm. He thinks it has something to do with his arm. But he's not sure which one or why.

There is a woman at the table. He is sure of that.

And he is in a kitchen.

He is sure of that, too.

Kitchens do not have drains in the center of the floor.

The cement block room outside Managua did not have windows, but it did have a drain.

You do not have to hose down a kitchen afterward.

First, though, you must ask the questions.

And to ask a true question, you must know what is true.

Otherwise, you are lost. Irrevocably lost.

That's why you have drains and uniforms. And why you must keep each clean.

Because nothing else is.

He winked, Ramon Delgado did.

The judge threw out the evidence and declared a mistrial, and Ramon Delgado, who thought the law was his toy, had picked up his files and then looked over at him from the defense table and winked.

Ramon Delgado did not understand that a thing is what it's named.

Wetback, for example.

Your back could be wet, but that did not mean you were clean.

There are no drains in a courtroom though.

That's why he needed matches.

A baker's dozen, including Delgado.

No winking, that time, when he locked the door in the safe house.

Borders. This side. That side.

Everything burns except the law.

That's part of what he's supposed to be remembering, something about the law, and his arm, his left arm, the one not cuffed to the pantry door, the arm he keeps lifting and throwing at his right ankle, like he's slowly waving the woman at the table over.

That's what cops do. Wave you over.

Then they ask you questions.

Except he's not a cop. Not anymore.

And he can't ask questions anymore either, because his tongue is swollen and bloated and slow and will not help him say the words.

But she gets up from the table anyway and crosses the room, and when she squats in front of him, he remembers.

Thanks to Jimmy Coates, he is not a cop anymore, but he has not forgotten how to think like one.

His left arm remembered. Now all of him does.

An unwritten law: no cop goes in without a throw-down.

His is strapped above his right ankle.

A Taurus auto-pistol, nine-shot magazine.

And this time his fingers find it.

She's starting to move out of her crouch, her head turning toward the door.

But he's already lifting his arm, following her, and just before he pulls the trigger, Aaron Limbe knows this: He has come to fullness and completion, and he will be forever in this moment.

The wood's so spongy around the clasp that Jimmy doesn't bother picking the lock on the shed; he simply pulls it off and levers the door, then steps inside and starts hunting down a shovel.

That might take a while though. The shed's crammed everywhere with junk, most of it his grandfather's, from back when the ranch and Gramps were still functioning, before he squandered his business holdings and finally over 1,800 acres of prime south Maricopa Valley on a string of wildcat investment schemes, waiting until he was seventy to undo what it had taken him forty years to build, the ranch dismantled parcel by parcel by the bank until it had shrunk to the house and twenty acres, and Gramps had retreated to a chaise lounge with red and white plastic webbing that he stationed behind the house so that he faced the skyline of the city and century that had outgrown and outfoxed him and worked his way through a handful of cigars and a fifth of bourbon a day, every day, for the last three years of his life, "dotting the i" he called it, and laughing, Jimmy remembering that laugh, long and deep, a laugh that always seemed somehow bigger and more complicated than the man himself.

Jimmy's surrounded by old cardboard boxes collapsing into each other and spilling magazines, dishes, and clothes, a couple of lawnmowers, a saddle and tack, a broken chandelier, a pile of kerosene lanterns, cans of paint and primer, an artificial Christmas tree, three fishing poles, toolboxes, a weathervane, and a handheld post-hole digger, but no shovel, so he picks his way further into the shed.

Portions of the roof and walls are missing, and the air's checkerboarded with floating pieces of light. Everything around him is dry-rotted, dust-covered, or rusted. He keeps expecting Evelyn to appear in the door behind him and admit that watching what sidewinder venom does to someone's nervous system was maybe not such a hot idea after all, but she doesn't show up, and all Jimmy wants is to get that grave dug and fast.

Jimmy spots the shovel in the far west corner of the shed. It's standing face up, a dusty ace of spades.

To get at it, he has to step around a galvanized washtub holding a dented mailbox and a pile of frayed rope, then drag a rusty set of bedsprings out of the way.

Jimmy leans over to grab the shovel, but stops when he sees he's about to step on a two-by-four with a large nail jutting from its center. He detours to the left instead.

And walks right into the web.

It takes him a couple seconds to realize that's what it is, a spider web, big as a bedsheet, because at first all that registers is the contact, the wrap and tangle where he'd been expecting air, and then he's flailing his arms and yelling, and no matter where he steps he's dragging part of the web with him, strands matting his hair and shirt, clinging to his eyelashes and lips and ears, and just as Jimmy's lifting his hands to his face, that's when he hears it, the abrupt punctuation of a pistol shot.

TWENTY-NINE

Jimmy's cycled through three days of visiting hours at Phoenix Memorial before he's finally alone in the room with Evelyn. The last couple of days have been wall-to-wall Scottsdale matrons, the country club and fitness center set, a parade of well-maintained thirty- and forty-somethings all trying to outdo each other in making empathy a fashion statement; and then there'd been Richard, the doting husband, Mr. Bedside Vigil, even the nurses talking about it, Jimmy overhearing them, what a fine man, how lucky Evelyn, etc., Jimmy left floating around the edges of the show until this afternoon.

Evelyn's propped up and asleep, an IV running into her left arm. There's a slight wheeze each time she takes a breath, and her color's gone south. She's lost some weight, it showing up first in her face, the cheekbones more insistent, sharpening the angles of her profile.

She turned her head.

That's what saved her life.

Simply that.

She turned her head, and the bullet hit the spot where shoulder and neck meet instead of ripping into her throat, a couple of inches that made all the difference.

She was lucky, the doctors said.

All Jimmy remembers, though, is the blood and Evelyn slumped against him as he hauled ass to the emergency room, Evelyn mumbling, saying something over and over that he couldn't catch, and bleeding, everything shrunken to a moment that held no room for luck or anything else except Jimmy's foot on the gas.

Then Richard had shown up, and Jimmy had wanted to wait around to see if Evelyn was going to be all right, but a gunshot victim brings out the cops and the cops have questions, and Richard was determined they'd get his answers, so Jimmy had driven back to his grandfather's house on West Dobbins and stood over Limbe's snake-bitten corpse, and then he'd scouted down the Smith & Wesson 3904, and he'd done what he couldn't do before, put a bullet in Limbe—two of them actually, one in the upper right thigh and the other a dead-center heart shot—and then he'd taken the cuffs off Limbe's wrist and left him propped against the pantry door and grabbed the canvas bag and left, Jimmy not bothering to wipe down for fingerprints because he could already see how things were going to play out, Richard putting in a call to one of his chamber of commerce or Rotarian or Jaycee buddies, and that buddy putting in a call to the commissioner or chief, and in the end you had an investigation that found what it was supposed to find, the version of events that Richard had worked out in the parking lot outside the emergency room with Jimmy, a simple case of self-defense, no incriminating batch of black-and-white photos, no murder for hire, no ransom demands, just Richard and Evelyn heading out to the farm to do some repair work and interrupting a burglary in progress, the guy panicking and shooting, hitting Evelyn, Richard running back to the car for the Smith & Wesson in the glove compartment, and the burglar ending up dead, with Jimmy spliced from the action altogether, as cleanly and neatly as his face had been from the photos Aaron Limbe had delivered to Richard.

The details on the books. Everything in place.

No need to dust for prints or look too closely at the corpse and push things with an autopsy. No need to run a check on the registration for the pistol that Richard supposedly owned and fired.

Or, for that matter, to work very hard at identifying the corpse, especially when that led back to a sociopathic ex-cop, a dead Mexican American lawyer, and a safe-house fire. That was some terrain the Phoenix police brass was not too keen on revisiting.

When the story hit the papers, it was buried in the back pages of the *Republic* and rated less than 150 words.

"Hey, Sleeping Beauty," Jimmy says, when Evelyn's eyelids flutter and finally open.

"Where's Richard?" Her voice is soft and raspy, still edged in sleep.

"Uh, the cafeteria, I think. He looked like he was headed that way when I came in."

"You don't know for sure?" She leans over, fumbling with the switch, and adjusts the top half of the bed into a sitting position.

"I didn't talk to him, Evelyn." Richard's a complication that Jimmy doesn't need right now. Jimmy had spent the greater portion of the afternoon ghosting the lobby, watching the elevator, waiting for Richard to leave the room. The last time they'd run into each other hadn't been pretty.

"He probably went for coffee," Evelyn says. "I know he must be tired. He spent the last two nights here, sleeping in a chair. Or trying to."

"Tell me about it," Jimmy says. "I've been hanging around, waiting for an opening."

Evelyn motions for the water glass, and Jimmy moves to the bedside stand, dumps in some ice, and fills the glass. Evelyn slips the straw between her lips and closes her eyes.

"I wake up so thirsty," she says between sips.

Jimmy steps closer and rests his hand in her hair.

She shakes her head from side to side. "No, Jimmy. Someone might see us."

He looks around and shrugs, then leans down and whispers, "I've missed you, honey." He steps back and lightly pats the front of his jeans. "Jimmy Junior has, too."

It takes a moment, and then Evelyn's smiling, but it's not the one he's used to. He pulls a chair over and sits down.

"A mess," Evelyn says, patting her hair. "I bet that's what I look like. Hand me my purse, will you?"

She rummages for a compact, flips it open, and frowns. "I'm going to get it cut as soon as I get out of here. Short. I've been wearing it too long." Evelyn digs around in the purse some more, comes up with a pack of breath mints, unwraps one, and slips it on her tongue.

"You look fine," Jimmy says. "I've always liked your hair long. It suits you."

"I'm too old to wear it that way. Shorter would be better." She pauses and looks at the door. "Did Richard say when he'd be back?"

"I didn't talk to him. I already told you that."

Evelyn takes another sip of water. The covers have slipped, and Jimmy's got a view, a nice one, of Evelyn's breasts shadowing her nightgown below the bandages on her right shoulder.

He slides the chair closer, reaching over and taking the hand with the IV patched on its back. "Everything's going to be all right," he says.

Evelyn nods. "Richard told me. He showed me the article in the *Republic.*"

"That, too," Jimmy says. "I was thinking more about Helena though. Leon's vet buddy, Frank Lawson, the guy who owns the bar, he's only going to hold the job for me two more days. The kidney stones, they're giving him problems again. I figure, to get up there in time, I better leave tomorrow morning." Jimmy pauses and nods, still moving the pad of his thumb up and down the back of Evelyn's hand. "Soon as the time's right, you can join me."

Evelyn picks up the breath mints, then sets them back down next to her purse. "The doctors say it may be awhile before I get my strength back."

"Fine. I'll be settled in by then." Jimmy goes on to tell her about the deal he's worked out with Lawson. The guy's got an apartment above the bar, supposed to be pretty nice, enough room for two people, and they can fix it up any way they want to.

Evelyn waits a beat too long to respond, and then all she says is, "Oh, Jimmy."

The way she says it brings him up short—Jimmy now knows what that phrase means—and she's looking everywhere but at him, and the longer it goes on, the more uncomfortable he is, because the thing is, she's not looking at him, but she's smiling, this wide-open smile, and he keeps hearing that *Oh, Jimmy,* the spin she put on it, and he wants to believe that smile is something that's been pumped through the IV, a pharmaceutical afterglow, but when she finally turns her head and looks at him, Jimmy's scared, plain flat-out scared, about what's coming next.

"Richard is a good man," she says.

Jimmy expects her to add something else, but she leaves it there, as if that news flash explained everything.

"He's a swell guy, Richard is, all right. A regular saint." Jimmy lets go of her hand and sits back in the chair, shaking his head. He points out the good man hired Aaron Limbe to kill him and almost got her killed in the process.

"He thought he was going to lose me," Evelyn says quietly.

"You know he blames me for you getting shot," Jimmy says. "That and the ransom. He thinks I took it."

Evelyn looks at the doorway and nods. She starts smoothing the bedcovers. She's got both hands going at the same time. Above her, the IV line twitches and jumps.

Jimmy can't get past the images tumbling around in his brain, Evelyn undressing, Evelyn undressed, a swarm of fingers, lips, nipples, and thighs, of flesh cupped and kneaded, parted and entered, and he can't shut them down or off or make the images match the woman lying in the hospital bed and what she's saying.

The room's squeezing him, too. Hospitals have always made him nervous, and everything here—from the low buzz of the fluorescents, the soft green and white floor and walls, the antiseptic air, the cut flowers and cards lining the windowsill and nightstand, to the television mounted high in the corner—everything unlocks an awkward mix of anger and panic in him.

"For a while there, I was confused," Evelyn says softly. "I was confused, and I did things, Jimmy. Things that I should not have done. They weren't me. You do that if you're confused. I did things, and he saw. He did. He saw what I was doing, and then he showed me what I did."

At first, Jimmy thinks she's referring to Richard. "Wait a minute," he says. "Limbe's dead. He can't do anything to you now. We're clear."

Evelyn looks down, tenting the top of the bedcovers, and then slips her hands beneath them.

"I wasn't myself," she says. "That's what happens when you're confused. You aren't yourself, and then you do things."

"Stop it, Evelyn. Okay? Stop."

Jimmy can't let it go, not now, not when they've finally got their chance and there's nothing to hold them back, when they've finally come through, and everything they'd talked about, he keeps telling Evelyn, it's right there in front of them, and all they have to do is take it.

"I've been married for almost half my life, Jimmy. What I did was foolish. I wasn't thinking. Or at least not clearly. I forgot who I was for a while."

"You're turning everything around, Evelyn. It's not that simple. It never was. Not even at first. But definitely not later. Not then. And not now."

Then Jimmy's massaging his temples and telling himself that it's the hospital, not Evelyn, talking. A hospital's no different from a principal's office or a police station or any other official space, the air itself shaping whatever you tried to say into something else. They were rooms with weight, like barometric pressure you could feel on your skin.

When Jimmy looks up, Evelyn's got that smile going again, the one that brought him up short earlier.

"Wait a second," he says. "What did you just say?"

"I said that Richard's forgiven me. The last couple of nights, we've done a lot of talking."

Jimmy's out of his chair and moving around the room, his

breath trapped high in his chest, but no matter where he puts his feet, he keeps running up against the open door of the hospital room, and he can't face the prospect of what lies outside it with no Evelyn, the idea of moving around a world with the heart torn out of it, no way that. No way.

"I'm not believing this," he says finally. And that's when he recognizes it, the smile, where he's seen it before.

It's her stewardess smile. The flight attendant special.

The one Evelyn brought home from her job on the airlines and transplanted for her spot in The Evelyn and Richard Show, the one Jimmy always associated with their storybook lives, a pleasant and friendly smile that went no further than itself and that always seemed to wear Evelyn instead of the other way around.

The same one she's resurrected now and hidden herself behind.

"I'm sorry, Jimmy," she says, adjusting the bedcovers. "I really am."

"Sorry and forgiven. That's some package deal, Evelyn."

He moves closer to the bed. She keeps the smile aimed at him. He reaches down and touches her cheek. "I'm going to tell him," Jimmy says softly. "I'm going to fucking well tell him."

He watches the smile waver. It's his last card.

"I'll tell Richard who's in the photos with you," he says, "and then we can see just how far Saint Richard's famous capacity for forgiveness can take him on that one."

Evelyn closes her eyes for a moment. Her hands are trembling. "He doesn't need to know that," she says.

Jimmy says he's not so sure about that.

He's thinking, he tells Evelyn, of setting the whole table. Lay everything out. Enlighten Richard, too, about exactly what happened to the ransom money he believes Jimmy took. He'll tell Richard how he gave the cash to Teresa Ruger and her family because Richard and Aaron Limbe killed her husband, that Don Ruger's blood is on both their hands because Richard hired Aaron Limbe to kill his wife's lover and Aaron Limbe missed and got Don instead, so Richard owes on that one; and Jimmy will tell Richard about how Aaron Limbe played him, cutting the face and head out of all those black-and-white eight-by-tens, suckering Richard in, so that Limbe could get paid for doing what he was going to do anyway, what he'd wanted to do for a long time, and that was to kill Jimmy, and Jimmy figures he'll pause there, let Richard soak up where things are headed, and then double-barrel him with the truth about whose face belonged on those black-and-whites with his wife.

"No," Evelyn says.

"What, no?" Jimmy asks.

She's still holding on to the smile. Jimmy can't get around or behind it.

"No, you won't tell Richard," she says. "You won't. I know you, Jimmy. You're a good man, too. You just haven't figured that out yet."

Jimmy's moving around the room again, clenching and unclenching his fists. The door to the bathroom is ajar, and in passing, he gets a glimpse of himself. He doesn't like what he sees. Not a guy centered in some solidly righteous anger, a guy who understood the mechanics of payback, a guy ready to balance the family books once and for all, no, none of the above, because Jimmy's thinking what he saw was a guy headed for the edge of a cliff, whose next step or the one after was going to be meeting nothing but air.

"At the farm, when you were teaching me how to shoot?" Evelyn asks.

Jimmy starts toward the bed, then stops.

"Do you remember what I said to you afterward?"

Jimmy shakes his head no. He remembers the afternoon heat, the targets in the orchard, him standing behind Evelyn, coaching her on how to breathe when she pulled the trigger, him leaning in, his hand on her wrist, and then Evelyn turning her head. He remembers the kiss, but not what she said after it.

" 'I'll decide if that happened or not.' That's what I said, Jimmy." Evelyn lowers her head, and Jimmy hears something tear in her breath.

"Wait a minute. Okay? Just wait." Jimmy is shaking. Everything's glass. "No way, Evelyn," he says, stepping toward her. "Maybe you said that. But it doesn't work that way. It just doesn't."

"Oh, Jimmy." The smile is gone, and she's looking right at him. "Sometimes it does. Sometimes it has to."

THIRTY

It's been a long fall.

Everyone in Helena says so. Autumn's kited a check that winter's pocketed and neglected to cash, the trees still holding their leaves and the leaves themselves in Crayola mode, clear light-filled days and color everywhere, the temperature unseasonably warm, the sky too big for the horizon.

Jimmy's tending at The Corner Place.

What he hears from his side of the bar and on the street is mostly talk about the weather. The inhabitants of Montana, like Arizona's, wallow in meteorological observations. People talk, and they talk about the weather. It's a safe, shorthand subject that stands in for any number of others, and under the right circumstances it generates its own drama and takes on the size and scope of history lessons.

Even though Helena and western Montana have always cut a better deal on weather conditions than the eastern portions of the state, as the new kid Jimmy is treated to dozens of stories about the legendary Montana winters, the wrath of ice, snow, and chinooks, of endless leaden skies and frozen pipes and frostbite, of tire chains and snowdrifts and dead batteries.

In the meantime, it's early November, and fall's still holding its breath, and The Corner Place is open for business. It's a shot-and-a-chaser kind of place, an old neighborhood bar, dark and quiet with wood-panelled walls and a long L-shaped bar, a few booths and a scattering of tables, a juke Jimmy is working on getting restocked, and a back room holding three pool tables and a bank of video poker machines.

The clientele's working class, men and women from the area plants manufacturing aluminum, drywall, or insulation, or from one of the mines or sand and gravel yards, or the meatpacking and diary-processing plants, and Jimmy's busiest at shift changes. He'll have them two or three deep at the bar then, the numbers gradually thinning out over the next hour to the regulars, those who are in no hurry to get home or see The Corner Place as one.

His boss, Leon Glade's old vet buddy, is an okay guy to work for. Unlike Leon, Frank Lawson has a sense of humor and more than one mood. Lawson's big and balding and sports a curly oversized pair of muttonchop sideburns, has four grown kids, three ex-wives, a well-stocked weekend getaway cabin in the mountains, and a vintage mint-condition Beechcraft Twin Bonanza. Besides The Corner Place, he owns or is a partner in a pizza joint, video store, and two car washes. From what Jimmy can tell, the only things that consistently knock Frank Lawson out of a good mood are Republican politicians and his recurring bouts of kidney stones.

Frank's about to be a grandfather again. His daughter over in Billings has been having a difficult pregnancy, and he's flown there to stay with her for a while, so for the last couple of weeks, Jimmy's been working like a regular citizen, putting in the overtime and after conferring with Lawson on the phone each afternoon, going on to pick up some of the slack in the managerial duties for running the bar.

Any other circumstances, Jimmy would've worked hard to duck that kind, or any kind, of work, but he's learning some of the citizens' secrets, one of which is if you work hard and stay busy, you don't have time to think, and that suits Jimmy just fine, the not thinking part, because when he does, nothing in his brain is his friend.

The nights, after closing, are the worst, Jimmy all loose ends in the apartment above the bar, no center to anything, no hand- or footholds around, everything painful, broken, and lost in his life flying in, coming at him from under the radar, each tick of the clock its own little cage, memory marking him—his father clutching his chest and losing control of the car as it hit the entrance ramp to Route 10, Don Ruger bleeding on him in a toy store parking lot, Aaron Limbe and his dead-end eyes, Evelyn with an IV patched into the back of her hand and lost in the stewardess smile, no chapter and verse or buyer protection plan to help out with any of that, Jimmy right up against it.

He's found out the empty hours after midnight take everything on their own terms.

Insomnia is a long hello. You get to meet your demons.

So each night, after closing, Jimmy rides things out the best he can, sitting in front of the television on a piece of lawn furniture, an old chaise lounge with frayed plastic webbing he found tucked away in the bar's storage room, Jimmy armed with an ashtray and lighter and some cold ones and watching old Westerns that he checks out earlier in the day from Lawson's video store.

Cowboy movies is what Jimmy had called them as a kid.

High Noon, Rio Bravo, She Wore a Yellow Ribbon, Stagecoach, My Darling Clementine, Gunfight at the OK Corral, The Magnificent Seven, The Left-Handed Gun, The Searchers, 3:10 to Yuma.

His favorites are *Shane* and *The Man Who Shot Liberty Valance.* Those are the ones he saves for the heart of his insomnia, the 3 A.M. viewings.

Then sleep, when it comes, if it comes, depending on his luck.

Once he's behind the bar again, Jimmy's okay. There's a routine to tending and a rhythm to that routine that smooth things out. Jimmy does not have to think too long about how Evelyn has never answered any of his letters or postcards. He does not have to remember a particular shade of lipstick or its taste or the lift and bend of a leg as Evelyn leaned back on a bed and peeled off a stocking. He does not have to think about the claims flesh makes upon flesh or about their hold on you.

What's left is Jimmy and the regulars at The Corner Place. Each day, the regulars settle in and hunker down, and it's his job to keep the drinks coming. The regulars like him. Jimmy's got the touch for drawing a draft right. He knows the art and physics behind a cold one—the proper temperature of the glass, the angle of the glass to the spout, the weight and pressure of the fingertips on the lever, the precise duration of the pull to produce the perfect head, which, if anyone asks, Jimmy will tell them it's five-sixteenths of an inch. Jimmy brings his in right on the money, and if proof is necessary, Jimmy will take out the wooden ruler he keeps behind the bar next to the box for the in-house sports bets and let you check it out for yourself.

Those at The Corner Place, like the regulars at any other small neighborhood bar, want a side order of talk or silence with their drinks. There are those who sit in front of their drafts with the thousand-yard stare and there are those who talk it up, complaining about the federal government, jobs, spouses, children, the conditions of the roads, the tax base, the cost of food, the fate of their favorite teams, or the weather; and Jimmy's come to figure out there's finally not much difference between the two, except in the noise level. What brings each group to the bar and keeps them there is what everybody else knows too—that things can curdle, shrink, dissolve, explode, expire, or disappear on you.

And sooner or later will.

But not end.

That's also what Jimmy's come to figure out from his side of the bar.

Nothing ends.

Nothing.

Liar's Night, that's what Jimmy has dubbed the second and last Fridays of each month at The Corner Place. There's something different in the air then. Friday's payday, and everyone's got the green. The regulars are restless. They plot and scheme and hatch plans. They revisit and revise their lives. They conjure possibility. Promise is their pal. Life's sweet. They have some money in their pockets, and the world's bigger all of a sudden. So are they. So, for a while, are their dreams.

On those nights, the place hops.

If you walk into The Corner Place on one of those Fridays, you'll find Jimmy, who's never been a big fan of the facts himself, behind the bar, and at some point in the evening, you'll see him take an empty tab sheet and fold it just so—right down the center so that the paper's tented—and he'll pull out a pen and block-letter RESERVED on each side of the sheet, and then he'll set the paper on the stool in front of his station and go back to levering drafts.

No matter how crowded the place is, none of the regulars bother the stool or Jimmy about sitting there.

If you ask around, someone will tell you it's saved for Jimmy's father.

Ask someone else, you'll hear it's reserved for Jimmy's good buddy Don Ruger.

A woman, this woman named Evelyn, is what you'll hear from someone else.

Of course, you could ask Jimmy himself. He'll pause, scratch his ear, look over at the door, and smile before answering.

Hey, he'll tell you, the bar's open. The beer's cold. You never know who might show up.

Lynn Kostoff is currently an associate professor of English at Francis Marion University in Florence, South Carolina, and is at work on his second novel, the first of a projected series featuring a Northern patrolman transplanted to the Myrtle Beach Police Department.